KĪPUKA

FINDING REFUGE IN TIMES OF CHANGE

ISBN 978-1-943756-05-6

This is issue #119 of *Bamboo Ridge,*
Journal of Hawai'i Literature and Arts (ISSN # 0733-0308).

Published by Bamboo Ridge Press

Printed in the United States of America

Bamboo Ridge Press is a member of the Community of
Literary Magazines and Presses (CLMP).

Editor: Juliet S. Kono

Guest editors: Donald Carreira Ching, Meredith Desha Enos,
Brenda Kwon, Misty-Lynn Sanico

Typesetting and design: Kristin Kaleinani Lipman

Cover art: *Mānoa, O'ahu* by Nanea Lum, 2020; canvas, earth, stone, and water process, carbon
ink, 'alaea earth pigment, rabbit skin glue, acrylic medium; 62" × 74"

Page 8 art: *Erasure* (detail) by Maika'i Tubbs, 2008; audiocassette magnetic tape
and casings, wire; 156" x 72" x 18"

Bamboo Ridge Press is a nonprofit, tax-exempt corporation formed in 1978 to foster the
appreciation, understanding, and creation of literary, visual, and performing arts by, for,
or about Hawai'i's people. This project was supported in part by grants from the National
Endowment for the Arts; the Hawai'i State Foundation on Culture and the Arts (through
appropriations from the Legislature of the State of Hawai'i and grants from the National
Endowment for the Arts); and the Cooke Foundation, Ltd. Additional support for Bamboo
Ridge Press activities provided by the Hawai'i Council for the Humanities.

Bamboo Ridge is published twice a year.
For orders, subscription information, back issues, and to purchase books contact:

Bamboo Ridge Press
P.O. Box 61781
Honolulu, Hawai'i 96839-1781
808.626.1481
read@bambooridge.org
www.bambooridge.org

5 4 3 2 1   21 22 23 24 25

CONTENTS

FROM THE EDITORS

Land changes. Gentrification, economic fluctuation, and urban sprawl transform Hawaiʻi's once-familiar territory into the unrecognizable. Most recently, Kakaʻako's revitalization disoriented residents as old landmarks were razed to give way to shops and high-rises. Ever-changing times make for ever-changing places. Wanderers in our own backyard, we learn and form new relationships to replacement geographies that can sometimes leave us longing for what has been lost.

This terrestrial palimpsest reaches further back than agricultural industries and tourism booms, further than the overthrow of the Hawaiian Kingdom. In Hawaiʻi, the ʻāina itself teaches us in its rawest, most powerful form that landscapes are created and recreated time and time again. Lava flows remind us how land is a living, dynamic force, not something inanimate that exists purely for our use. Kīlauea's 2018 eruption demonstrated the natural law of erasure and renewal, as well the ʻāina's power of birth with the formation of Lōʻihi, the newest island in the chain.

If nothing is static and everything changes, in what can we anchor? Are we always at the mercy of our environment? Does the idea of "home" inherently imply that the words "for now" follow?

Little did we know that these questions would be more relevant than we could ever have imagined. We began this project at the end of 2019 when the word "coronavirus" carried a vague threat of calamity we couldn't quite fathom. In 2020, that calamity swept the Earth as the number of deaths steadily ticked higher in figures that shocked some and inspired denial in others. Designated workers jeopardized their lives in emptied landscapes in the name of what was "essential" while much of society learned the terrain of their households with an unwelcome familiarity. Those with nowhere to go remained on quiet streets, waiting for COVID. Our new surroundings gave rise to everything from an increase in domestic violence and mental illness to recipes for sourdough bread. Wildlife crept out of hiding, turning cities into jungles and oceans into playgrounds. The world was no longer as we knew it.

With nowhere to run, we watched Minneapolis police officer Derek Chauvin murder George Floyd with a knee to his neck. Those eight minutes and forty-six seconds shook the world with outrage and #blacklivesmatter as then-President Donald Trump ordered protestors to be tear-gassed, pepper-sprayed, and shot with rubber bullets so that he could take a photo in Lafayette Square. As time marched forward toward a contentious election and historic "firsts," weapon-wielding insurgents stormed the Capitol and casualties resulted in the name of voter fraud. Our elected were sworn into office, and as much as we loved that our Vice President was a woman of Black and South Asian descent, celebratory remarks turned into voices of protest as hate crimes against Asians rose by triple digit percentages. The mythic bearers of "the China virus" and the "kung flu," Asians learned to expect anything for the crime of existing: beatings, stabbings—even a mass shooting.

In the midst of such unprecedented upheaval, where do we find stability? More than mere steadfastness, constancy is the life preserver towards which we swim. It holds our survival.

When volcanoes erupt, variances in topography create kīpuka, islands of turf untouched by the flow of lava. While Pele's fiery rivers caress its borders, its plants and seeds remain. It watches lava cool, then blacken. It witnesses pāhoehoe break down into rich volcanic soil. And when the time comes, it seeds its surroundings, sets free former boundaries as genesis and legacy join. Nā kīpuka preserve and regenerate. They survive and persist. They anchor and hold life, ensuring in the end that nothing is forgotten.

It is in this spirit of what holds us in times of change that we present to you the work of writers and artists who explore and engage where kīpuka lies for them.

Donald Carreira Ching
Meredith Desha Enos
Brenda Kwon
Misty-Lynn Sanico

MARK K. ANDERSON

TO FERNANDO

I.

To Fernando
The dove who flies to my feet each morning
When I open the screen door
And step outside onto the lanai to feed the koi
You do know
My aim is better than what you see
I deliberately miss the pond
With some of the pellets I toss to the koi
So the pellets will bounce off the rocks
And into the deep grass (that I have been meaning to cut)
Those pellets are for you, Fernando
You must know that by now
I prefer feeding you this way
To preserve your dignity

II.

Can I say?
I admire how you have learned
To hold onto the rocks that surround the pond
using that claw of a foot you have
To reach far into the pond
to pluck pellets off the swirling surface
Wings flapping, water splashing, but your balance kept

III.

Please be careful!

If you were to fall into the pond, could you get out?
I wonder
And please know the koi do not like you for stealing their food
They have told me this
I would not trust them

IV.

Can I ask you?
Where do you go during the day?
Is it to Chinatown?
If so, please be careful
There are many homeless
Birds in Chinatown
Don't make eye contact with them
They can become suddenly violent
Ignore their sad looks
And false signs
Many are not from here
Everything has been tried to help them
Nothing works

V.

If you do go to Chinatown during the day
Can I ask you to wash your feet before you come back?
Before you wet them in the pond
The koi already do not like you
And if they knew where your feet have been
They will like you even less
If you need me to leave you out a bowl of water
Let me know
I am happy to do this

VI.

But really I am writing all this to ask you
Can you please send me word of what happened?
If for some reason
You decide not to return one day
Otherwise I will always wonder
    And hope to see you
    When I open the screen door

AMALIA B. BUENO

PERLA AND HER LOVELY BARBIE

I told my younger sister Perla that she should not love Barbie so much. I never loved Barbie when I was her age. I didn't even like Barbie. She didn't look real to me. Her big blue eyes so empty and cold scared me. I didn't like Barbie's skinny legs, too. They reminded me of how short and ugly my brown legs are. In fact, nobody in my family looks like Barbie. None of my cousins, none of my neighbors, nobody in my homeroom class looks like her. Nobody in my whole school—except for Elizabeth Watson—she looks full-on haole like Barbie.

Now that Perla is 8 and I'm 12, we were old enough to do special things to Barbie, I told Perla. When she asked what kind of things, I said like giving Barbie a hot bath in very hot water. But Perla wouldn't do it. Even when I said that I wouldn't really boil the water, just make it very hot on the gas stove upstairs. I even told Perla I would bring the pot under the house where we played so that nobody would see us. A hot bath wouldn't hurt Barbie because her skin is very hard, I said. But Perla wouldn't believe me. She didn't want to be part of the experiment to see if Barbie's skin would slowly get soft or if it would melt right away.

The Barbie doll that Perla plays with used to belong to our older sister Marina, who goes to high school now. She's 16 and doesn't want anything to do with us anymore. She tries to ignore us, but we like to keep up with whatever is going on in her life. Marina had only one Barbie. Marina passed that Barbie on to me when I was six. I passed her straight on to Perla, who was only two years old at the time. Perla loved that Barbie more and more each year, even though she was given other Barbies by our relatives. This year I noticed that Perla was starting to act more and more like Marina. Like wanting to wear dresses instead of pants and eating less and smiling more. Perla also didn't want to go outside and play in the sun as much, because she didn't want her skin to get darker. Just like our sister Marina, who always put on sunscreen and wore a hat even if it wasn't sunny outside.

I would usually be spending more time with my best friend Joshua, but he is in summer school for the first time. Me and Joshua used to go everywhere after school and during the summer. We played war games under the house, explored the neighborhood streets and drainpipes, caught the Ala Moana bus to the beach by ourselves, and set up camp in his backyard for sleepovers and scared each other by telling spooky stories. But Joshua is taking pre-algebra and band classes this summer. Elizabeth Watson, the only pure haole girl in our school, is in Joshua's band class. And even though he won't admit it, I think Joshua is in love with Elizabeth. I told him last week I was tired of hearing about Lizby this and Lizby that and Lizby said this and Lizby did that. I noticed Joshua's ears turned red when I was saying those things, so that's when I knew he liked her.

And what kind of name is Lizby, I asked? He didn't answer. Her name sounds like a type of lizard, I laughed. I made my voice sound like the *National Geographic* guy on TV and announced, "The Lizby type of gecko lives in Kalihi Valley and plays the flute in the summer." I was only teasing, but Joshua didn't laugh. He didn't say anything to defend her and he didn't say anything back to me, which made me feel funny. So I told him that Elizabeth Watson looks just like a stiff Barbie doll.

Now Joshua hardly comes over any more. When he does, he is really polite and doesn't want to do anything that will get his clothes dirty or make him sweaty. I miss Joshua and the things we used to do. When I'm bored and there's nothing to do, I hang out with Perla.

One day me and Perla were downstairs under the house, our favorite play spot. Perla was brushing Barbie's hair. Barbie had her Silken Flame outfit, the "1998 reauthorized edition" the box said. Her clothes, even if they were almost seven years old now, looked okay except that the white satin skirt had little brownish streaks in some places. The red off-the-shoulder silk top fit over Barbie's big cheechees like a tube top, only it was shaped like McDonald's M's in front. The gold purse and gold belt had some of the shiny stuff come off in some places, but it still looked nice. The black shoes were still good.

Perla put Barbie in her make-believe bed. When she noticed I was playing with matches, she came over to help me. I had found some pieces of our Lola's dried tabako leaves that she left on top of her old Singer sewing machine, preparing to roll them into her fat cigars. Perla watched me twist a small piece of tabako, light it, and twirl the leaf to make spiral smoke. We did this for a little while until it got boring. I told Perla we should stop already because Lola would probably smell the tabako pretty soon and come down and scold us. So we looked for some other things to burn.

We dug a small hole in the ground and decided to push the stinkbugs into it using the lighted end of the matchsticks. But the stinkbugs would only dig deeper in the hole and go under the dirt. This gave me an idea. I convinced Perla that we should pretend we were at a funeral. We made the hole bigger and looked for things to put inside. I told Perla to go look around the yard for any dead animals. I went upstairs to get some chicken bones from the kitchen trash can.

When I came back to the hole, Perla was already there and she told me she didn't find any dead animals so she got rotten mangoes from the ground and picked white plumerias with brown edges. I told her to go look for some white rocks to line the sides of the hole while I would make a cross with some Popsicle sticks. We arranged the bones like a whole chicken and buried it. We carefully covered the bones with a thin layer of dirt and put some small gray rocks around the edges because Perla couldn't find any white ones. We put our palms together, kneeled down on our cardboard mat and said an Our Father.

Perla said we should do a novena even though we didn't know how to say the Filipino words. I agreed. We pretended we had just finished the ninth night of prayer and was doing the ending part called Santa Maria, Santa Maria, Santa Maria. I told Perla that I would be the priestess leader and she could be the audience and repeat after me. "Santa Maria, napno ka ti gracia ni Apo Dios," I said it very fast and very serious and very sing-songey. Perla copied me. Next I said, "Saint Mary, napno ka ti paria and apple juice." Perla laughed when she realized that the Virgin Mary was full of bitter melon and apple juice. But Perla wouldn't repeat after me. I said the Filipino version three times, then the mixed English version three times. I ended with, "Mother Mary, you are full of bitter melon" and pushed the cross in at the far end where the chicken's head was buried. Perla gasped, surprised at the force I had to use because the dirt was hard.

We dug another hole and put in four rotten mangoes and five dead plumerias. We used the leftover dirt we had from digging the chicken's grave and made a burial mound of dirt like an imu. The dead mangoes and dead plumerias were double dead now. Three big mango leaves straight up in the middle of the mound completed the graveyard scene. I pushed the stems of three fresh plumerias in front of the long green leaves. It looked like a happy mound.

Then I had an idea.

I told Perla wouldn't it be fun to dress Barbie up in nice clothes and then bury her for a few days? Perla didn't want to. At first. I told her, Perla Conchita Domingo Asuncion, you said so yourself that you do real things to Barbie, like feed her, and sing to her and comb her hair. Well, I explained, another real thing that happens is people go away and people die. We could practice burying Barbie as just another real thing that people do. We could pretend Barbie died, say a Mass for her and then bury her. Perla still didn't want to.

So I said we could dig Barbie up nine nights later. I could tell Perla was thinking about it. So, I said, as a bonus, on the tenth day we could pretend that one whole year had gone by and we could have a one-year death anniversary party for Barbie. After that, Perla smiled and said okay. But only if we dressed Barbie really nice and gave her all the things that you are supposed to put inside a coffin. To that, I responded with a big grin, "Of course. No probe-lem-ma."

We were going to make sure that Barbie got everything she needed to live in heaven. I made a list of all the necessary stuff that has to go inside a coffin: money, soap, toothbrush, toothpaste, shoes, change of clothes, non-gold jewelry, needle and thread, wallet, comb, slippers, socks, sleeping clothes.

I hunted around in our mommy's clothes drawers and finally found a small, shiny, black satin handkerchief. It was too small to cover all of Barbie but it would cover her from the waist down. The black would look nice against her red top, I thought. I found a dollar bill in Daddy's ashtray of loose change. I found a new toothbrush in the medicine cabinet. I put a little toothpaste on it so that I wouldn't have to take the whole tube of toothpaste. Perla brought down Barbie's pajama set and pink plastic shoes. She also took a pair of shorts and a T-shirt set from her California Girl Suntan Barbie. We borrowed a pair of fake silver and diamond earrings that Marina didn't use anymore. We knew she wouldn't miss it because she left it on the crowded bathroom counter. We found a needle and some thread in Lola's sewing machine drawer. The only thing we needed was socks.

I told Perla that since this was Hawai'i, we didn't need any socks because Barbie was going to Hawai'i heaven where it was warm all year. But Perla insisted and would not bury Barbie without sending her off with a pair of socks. I told Perla the container was too full already and if we added one more item then it would look like Barbie was suffocating. Perla wouldn't accept my explanation and said that it was her doll and she could bury her Barbie any way she wanted. Ugh, I hate when she gets all stubborn like this. I went upstairs to think. I knew she still wanted to play.

When I returned under the house where Perla was waiting, I had brought a larger, round Tupperware container and one tiny bootie that used to belong to our 2-year-old brother, Marcelino, who didn't fit them anymore. I hoped this would satisfy Perla's need for socks and it did, especially when I said that one bootie would keep both of Barbie's feet warm at the same time.

While Perla dressed Barbie in her Silken Flame outfit and arranged all the coffin items inside the Tupperware coffin, I dug a round hole with the shovel my grandpa kept in the corner tool shed next to the avocado tree. When it was deep enough, I lined the hole with one of daddy's old stained T-shirts, which I found lying around in the garage. He used it as a rag, so I figured nobody would miss it. I was already calculating how much or how little trouble I would get into for each of the missing items.

We buried Barbie by doing all the serious things we saw adults do at a funeral. I said a few words about how much happiness she brought to Marina, and Perla, and many girls around the world. Perla said how much she loved Barbie and how she wished to be like Barbie when she grew up. Then Perla pretended to cry and chant and howl like how the old Filipino women do at funerals. I started laughing but stopped when Perla gave me the stinkiest eye I ever got from any six-year-old. I joined her in the howling and chanting about Ken, about Barbie's parents, about the Mattel company, and how we would all be together soon.

For the next nine days we were supposed to wear black and pray. We decided that as long as we had something black on us, like a piece of black thread hanging over the waistband of our shorts, it was okay. We also decided that it was okay to laugh out loud, to go out to play with our friends, to sweep the floor, and to watch television comedy reruns like *Gilligan's Island*. We made our own rules because it was our funeral. And we got to decide how much the relatives of the dead person should be sad or relieved or happy or worried about money.

On the ninth day, Marina asked us if we had taken her new toothbrush. Our mommy had already asked about her satin handkerchief and I had to pretend I only saw a white scarf in the living room. Our Lola had also asked us about a needle she was sure she left in her sewing machine drawer. We were planning to put everything back on the tenth day after we dug Barbie up and finish having her one-year death anniversary party.

The next day, exactly 10 days after the burial, Marina asked if we had seen her earrings. It just so happened that me and Perla answered her at the exact same time, using the exact same words, "No, we didn't see it." That was probably why Marina didn't believe us. She threatened to tell our dad something about us digging a big hole under the house, her missing toothbrush and earrings, and a Barbie doll she hadn't seen Perla play with in over a week. Marina is so boring. Just because she's in high school, it doesn't mean she can't have fun with us anymore.

After we dug up Barbie, we didn't feel like having a one-year death anniversary party. Perla was disappointed that Barbie did not seem that pretty anymore. And her beautiful clothes were a little dirty. After not playing with Barbie for more than a week, she didn't seem to miss her as much as she thought she would. Now Perla mostly puts Barbie up on the shelf by her bed.

Perla takes Barbie down once in a while to let Barbie sit quietly next to her. I knew she would end up not loving Barbie so much. 🌿

ALLISON FRANCIS

SECOND WIFE

I know who he once was: a Japanese paniolo with a cruel lip and a
back in collapse. His feet are too forgiving from nightly massages
with kukui nut oil and fine sand fingers thick stiff gnarled by the
rope he grasps too tightly. They whispered to me—he was so cruel—

Women quickly turned away when he looked at them. They
whispered to me—just one glance from his pinched eyes could cut
your cheek, feel like the sting of his broad black rawhide.

I know what he once was. A keen rifleman, a lone centaur brooding
on black lava ridges swift nightrider crossing stone bridges daily
leaving behind ghosts of ranch hands.

He is hiding from me now but I know I know. I smell power fear
in his sweat when he rises each day. He rinses in cold water and
scrubs off my scent with a small horsehair brush. We will cross
Pāhoa this morning. I will watch the clay give way beneath his
steel-leathered steps. He will touch my cheek softly thick, gloveless
finger marking me with red dust.

Now, I will hide what I know underneath my parched straw hat
and coarse cotton blouse.

Tonight   I will bow then steal the curl of his lip.

Tonight   because I know who and what he once was I
              will remember to love him for the motherland he
              has lost.

ALLISON FRANCIS

YELLOW ROOSTER

"Tossing over old lovers like worn out slippas!"
Auntie yelled, fire sparking her teeth,
as yellow rooster posed like an arrow on the rock wall.
Tears hidden behind worn eyelids,
felt like hot lava or yesterday's spit.

Uncle didn't turn his head nor swing his
machete, striding like superman without a cape.
The knot at his spine loosened, then struck
his heels when he left—
coiling heat mourning a new loss.

Sweeping the red earth with her good eye,
she expected yellow rooster to crow
a slow victory, but all she heard was
his passing—
now he would be no more.

TOM GAMMARINO

DYSTOPIA IN PARADISE

"And if ever, by some unlucky chance, anything unpleasant should
somehow happen, why, there's always soma to give you a holiday
from the facts." -Aldous Huxley, *Brave New World*

A quick search on the word "paradise" in the online Yellow
Pages for Honolulu pulls up 269 businesses, among them Sushi
Paradise, Picnics in Paradise, Paradise Eyewear, Paradise Rent-
A-Car, Paradise Jerky, Cheeseburger in Paradise, Paradise
Barbershop, Paradise Carpet & Tile, Paradise Thai Massage,
Paradise Tanning, Paradise Media Group, Paradise Auto
Specialists, Paradise Ice, Paradise Lua (toilets), Paradise Dollar
Store, even Paradise Mortgage, as if that weren't a contradiction
in terms. The same search on my hometown of Philadelphia pulls
up 143 businesses, but since those results encompass a metro area
with over six times the population of the entire island of Oʻahu, the
disparity is telling, if not exactly surprising. Everyone knows that
paradise is what tourists come to Hawaiʻi for; I'm not sure anyone
has ever traveled to Philadelphia for that.

If tourists on Oʻahu ever leave the three-mile stretch of beach
called Waikīkī, it's generally to go snorkeling in Hanauma Bay or
maybe shopping in Haleʻiwa, the surfer's Shangri-La on the North
Shore. Perhaps they visit Pearl Harbor, hike Diamond Head, or
attend a lūʻau at Paradise Cove. Odds are sharply against their
venturing to the leeward side of the island, where they'd be forced
to reckon with the tent cities that "house" many of Oʻahu's five
thousand homeless people. And there's approximately no chance
that they'll take the time to learn the difficult history of these
islands—from missionaries bringing their creeds and pandemics, to

sugar magnates and foreign politicians illegally annexing a sovereign nation and placing a beloved queen under house arrest; to military occupation, overdevelopment, human-trafficking, a meth pandemic, a housing shortage, and the ongoing extinction of countless species.

And who can blame them? Most of these tourists don't come here to be in Hawai'i so much as "Hawaii," the paradise that exists foremost in their minds. "Hawaii" is a reward for all the time they've clocked working in their techno-industrial metropolises, an exotic pastoral from the "real" world, and as long as they keep forking over dollars, they can stay in that virtual-reality program as long as they like, gawking at fire-dancers and drinking from coconuts.

I teach Aldous Huxley's dystopian novel *Brave New World* in my Science Fiction class at a private high school in Honolulu. I usually begin by asking students who among them would like to live in the blissed-out, instant-gratification society Huxley conjures in his novel. In a class of twenty, about eighty percent say no. Even if I could wipe their memories so that they knew nothing of the world they were leaving behind, they want to believe they would despise living in such a place. "But guaranteed happiness!" I say. "And soma, the perfect drug with no side effects!"

The two or three students who didn't do the reading raise their eyebrows, but my provocations fail to move any of the nays. I push to learn what values these students prioritize over happiness, and they say things like "Meaning," or "It's all about the struggle." Some want to distinguish between bodily pleasure and true happiness. I ask if they don't think these are just the sorts of things unhappy people might say if they were trying to justify their way of being to themselves; they confess it's possible. On the other hand, I wonder if I might get different answers were I teaching students in different geographic and/or socio-economic contexts. How much struggle can a person take before faith in the redemptive value of suffering begins to erode? These are not rhetorical questions, but I don't know the answers.

At this point I usually draw a connection to *The Matrix*. In that film, Neo faces a choice between the red pill and the blue pill—that is, living in the "real world," where happiness is far from guaranteed, or in a satisfying simulation. Insofar as the analogy to *Brave New World* holds, my students are consistent: nearly all of them want the red pill.

Then I strip away the science-fiction trappings and recall a conversation I once had with a stranger on a plane. Let's say you've been married twenty years and couldn't be happier. Now, let's say your partner has been secretly meeting with your best friend four days a week for nineteen of those years. Do you want to know that?

The red-pill contingent, more or less to a person, say they would want to know. They value truth over happiness, they say. Some part of me wants to claim that in my forty-something wisdom I've come to understand that happiness is hard won and as long as I'm smiling, leave me be. After all, physicists tell us most of the universe is made up of dark matter and dark energy and we know almost nothing about those; what's one more little unknown about the universe? But that's bad faith. When push comes to shove, I too would want to know, would still subordinate happiness to the pursuit of aligning my life inasmuch as possible with objective reality. If I'm going to live inside a mental construct premised on a fiction—a simulacrum, virtual reality, soma holiday—then I at least want to know that.

Brave New World suggests that utopia is always in the eye of the beholder, but that doesn't keep Huxley from rhetorically implying judgment of his utopians' false consciousness. The central tension for Huxley, as signaled by the novel's epigraph, is between freedom and perfection. If those are mutually exclusive, which do you want? Before rushing to judgment, recall that, as world-controller Mustapha Mond reminds us, freedom necessarily encompasses "the right to grow old and ugly and impotent; the right to have syphilis and cancer; the right to have too little to eat; the right to be lousy; the right to live in constant apprehension of what may happen to-morrow; the right to catch typhoid; the right to be tortured by unspeakable pains of every kind."

And what about those twenty percent of my students who have no desire to be martyrs for truth, the blue-pill-poppers who subordinate all other values to happiness? My hope, perhaps naïve, is that this is a false binary, that as social creatures, our own happiness depends upon the flourishing of our communities, and my hedonistic students are simply too young to have had their beliefs tested in the field. I submit that one calculus for determining how posthuman we are *not* is to invoke the degree to which the suffering of others still cuts into our own happiness.

Alas, Ursula K. Le Guin's much-anthologized short story "The Ones Who Walk Away from Omelas" suggests I am indeed naïve. In the story, the happiness of a utopia depends on everyone's knowing that a malnourished, naked child sits in excrement in a dark cellar beneath their splendid city. Nearly everyone goes with the program, accepting the sacrifice of the "wretched one" as a necessary evil—the analogy to hypercapitalism seems obvious—but if I'm naïve, I'm at least not alone: occasionally a citizen of Omelas, rejecting the social contract, walks out of Omelas for good. Rousing though that citizen's resistance is, however, I can't help thinking mere conscientious objection is a copout, a sort of denial or virtue-signaling that in fact does nothing to ease the child's suffering or uproot the sadism (or schadenfreude?) of the society that depends on it. N.K. Jemisin offers a complex rebuttal to Le Guin's story with her own "The Ones Who Stay and Fight." In the author's (tweeted) words, the story is "an argument for action, rather than complacency or escapism, in the face of injustice. Interpret it however you like."

To be sure, a hundred and twenty-seven years after annexation, Hawai'i is too complex to admit of easy solutions to the legacy of Empire. It's easy enough for me to write critically of unreflective tourists, but the truth is, I struggle every day with my own identity as a non-native teacher in Hawai'i, and with what it means, or should mean, for me to love this place as I do. Should I be the spoilsport who attempts to disabuse vacationers of the belief that they're enjoying themselves? Given that tourism is Hawai'i's top industry, I'm honestly not sure; but then capitalism may well be the root of the problem. In any case, a recent back-and-forth in the media seems to me instructive. On June 28, 2019, *The New York Times* published an article on race in Hawai'i bearing the unfortunate title "Want to Be Less Racist? Move to Hawaii." In her response on her blog, scholar Akiemi Glenn included an image of the article redacted by community members on social media. The new title read "Want to Be Less Racist? Visit Hawai'i, Learn from Hawai'i, Contribute to Hawai'i, Then Please Leave Hawai'i (Unless you are willing to commit to help repair, restore, and regenerate our peoples and places...then we can begin a dialogue)." As every tourist knows, "aloha" means "hello," but as in Queen Lili'uokalani's most famous song, "Aloha 'Oe," it also means "goodbye."

Maybe, sometimes, walking away is the best way to stay and fight? 🌺

GLOSSARY FOR A STORM

F

fish (noun) · place two crabs in a bucket to see what she must become to survive. In the after, she is more gill than breath, more laughter than heart, two chambers instead of four, always preparing for a gust of wind to become a storm.

G

ghost (noun) · a conjuring that comes from a damaged body; a reconfiguration, of the living, a desire that becomes a damage or, what licks its fingers, bites its own nails, swallows stones; in the face of reconciliation she will spit out her own tongue, a refusal to stop its own form of resolving. *See definition of* haunt.

girl (verb) · pulled from weeds, still blooming, smelt and eaten with salt & vinegar, stuck between snaggletooth rocks, coveted, curated, traveled, remade-from-plastic, classified by size, arranged, made public, sold, made wild, again, melted down, to metal shanks, revenged, avenged, wrecked, wrought, weighed, wonted—a desire yet to be seen.

H

haole (noun) · the cleaving between settler and haunting; the shadow passing over the freeway on a clear day; a curse hitching a ride to Old Pali Road, repelled by blood and raw pua'a; what visits for two days, for five days, for a month; a romanticized escapist fantasy, a sunburnt menace, the none-otherwise-specified body, also known as half-lander, or pale skin chasing tradition. *See definition of* origin.

haunt (verb) · to echo; to scare yourself back into skin, a slick groan, a story that is your mother's too, a single beat, the time it takes, for a body to, splinter, a ritual of holding breath, at night, when you wipe down the counters with bleach and his blood. *See definition of* ghost.

> ex. I don't want to haunt you, but I
> already have.

home (noun) · a roughness between, mauka and makai, between rock and a foreign place like the crushed plastic run smooth, like what gets left out on the beach, jimmy boy's slippah and a few beer cans, what the ocean swallows, or spits out, like if you place a rock on the shoreline and it does not get washed away; what remains.

I

island (noun) · a geographically isolated body; a single storm blowing shrill, like a plastic whistle; a belly that feeds mountains, the nēnē bird flying east to west; a concrete mouth; a gasoline river traveling from valley to sea; a city of immigrants, a city of refugees; a city with missing natives, trapped inside a can of rusted spam.

M

mercy (verb) · once, during a tsunami advisory my sister and I hiked to the top of Koko Head Crater with binoculars and watched the tides suck on the wind, it kind of looked like pulling the lips back to reveal a set of teeth; and still when our parents asked "what did you see" all we could say was "water," which is to say to become the first breath before a storm, the gift a ghost grants you, even if it's not really a gift, but just the illusion of it.

O

---

origin (noun) · of daughter, of sister, of mother, of nuclear, family, of homeland, we do not visit, born from wine, bathed in chicken broth, raised among pencil shavings, of typewriter dust, of mango, the romance in coconut surf wax, of ashes, buried in the backyard, of the things I never met, never held, of holding space for a stillness, a way of being of, you, and so also of me. *See definition of* haole.

S

---

sex (adjective) · once, he took me without warning, once, he took me without reason, I searched the hook of my body for answers, for months I pulled him and each other man from me, a spool of silk nets, I tangled them into knots, around my fingers, a web, yes, uh-huhs, please, stop, no, thank you, no, I pulled my consent from my body and knitted song after song—

JOANNA GORDON

FROM

Kohelepelepe. Maunalua. Seconds shore break. From China
Walls to Sandys. The rickety two-story that guards Kalaniana'ole
Highway. From Ko'olau. From the sitting water tower. Looks like a
dragon eye on Koko Head. From the No. 1 bus. Crippling debt and
six-dollar milk. From imported goods. Taxes. Forest freeways and
homelessness. Settler colonialism steeped in chicken stock. Kill
haole day. From archives. Silverfish speckled atop newspapers.
From dining tables polished to a sheen. Jewish moms. Who cook
their pain into something extravagant. Pot roast. From salt. Garlic
and cutting coupons. From a body let down. From splintering
love. Mango trees that age into mango pie. Butter mochi. From
cockroaches scuttling into cupboards. Tropical storms. Humid
depressions. High winds. From settler. From daughter. From girl.
From homesick. From O'ahu. From.

JOANNA GORDON

MIGRATION

We came by boat, by plane. We came in droves and droves. We came for vacations, for plastic tropics, for coconut-flavored grandeur. We arrived as tourist and never left. We brought our husbands, our wives, our children. We came on fighter jets in fresh Navy whites. We chased our children with thick white sunscreen down beaches we couldn't pronounce—Wae-kiki and Ala Moena. We came in elaborate bathing costumes, all polyester frills and red & white bunting. We adorned our shoulders with lavish plumeria, with fragrant puakenikeni, with violet orchid lei. More names we can't pronounce; we call them flowers. Paradise is two dollars, made by nimble fingers we don't have to remember. We tell our children don't stare, don't talk to locals. We aren't sure if they speak the language we do, where that accent comes from, that skin with its dark wood stain, its wind-beaten working class look. We drink rum poolside at resorts called "The Royal Hawaiian" and call ourselves Hawaiian too. Sometimes we go home, swearing to call our Hawaiian romances, our lovely hula girls, and never do. Later we will reminisce about our exotic lovers, all hips and grass skirts. Sometimes we marry the hula girls, give them pale-faced children and last names like Smith. We buy land, buy homes, buy hotels. We hire locals to wash our floors and change our sheets for fifty cents a day. Elvis Presley vacations in our suites so we name a cocktail after him, a Blue Hawaii, blue curacao and pineapple juice, a moon sitting atop the weary sea.

JOANNA GORDON

WAITING FOR RAIN

Mom still hangs her laundry out to dry,
slippahs ankle deep in suckling grass

Dad cleans the rain gutters pulling
out the soggy plumeria leaves by hand

The girls finger the pages in their books restlessly,
Why can't we make a slip-n-slide? they whine

The dog wags its tail hoping
the sliding door will squeak open

While auntie who lives at the bus stop
huddles under her tarp-house for warmth

Tomorrow, the mountain will melt
its shoulders sliding downhill

and together in the rain, we
will all choke
on mud.

IN THE VALLEY

Uncle Jimmy had one house. Got koa wood floors, surfboards

We lost it all in mud　　　　　　　　　　*We lost it all in mud*

We lost signed and glassy mounted on the door.
it all in mud

Tyler bought three trucks—all with monster wheels—we thought

　　　　*We lost it all in m**We** lost it all in mud*

they could chew trees.　　　　　　*We lost it all in m**We** lost i*

Hoku had a lo'i patch. She buried her sisters deep in the valley and

lost it all in mud　　*We lost it all in mud*　　　　*We lost it all in mud*

kalo grew.　　*We lost it all in mud*

Uncle Ken got one chicken coop, called them Ronnie, Ku'ulei, and

　　　　　　　　　　　　　　We lost it all in mud

Pickle-head.　　*We lost it all in mud*

　　　　　　　　　　　　　　　We lost it all in mud

　　We lost it all in mud

Mr. & Mrs. Otsuka at the end of the road watched over us from

　　　　　　　*We lost it all in m**We** lost it all in mud*

their house on stilted legs all pointed fingers and expectant sighs. *We lost it a*

When the wind blew, they swayed over the ridge.

We lost it all in mud　　　　　　*We lost it all in mud*

We lost it all in mud

The Fujiokas had mango trees sweet as Kool-Aid sick and mottled

　　　　We lost it all in mud

tree sap. They swished their tree tails and craned necks into the

　　　　　　　　　　　　We lost it all in

We lost it all in mud

Soongs' backyard, the family old as lychee trees. Tart and gnarled

We lost it all in mud

skins, bruised and knotted over a cracked sun. The Foxes had the

We lost it all in mud

four-car garage we all like get. When walking our dogs, we pause in

We lost it all in m

front of it, letting them sniff a bit longer.   We lost it all in mud

With

ı mud

hopeful mouths we chewed on its shiny doors and say *someday*. The

Tanakas got cinderblock walls so high we never saw the front door

but smelled it— strawberry and ginger, flour and red bean. Kea was

We lost it all in mud
blind and always losing his cat, calling through the streets *Anu,*
We lost it all in mud   We lost it all in mud
Anu. We each took turns feeding him dried tuna and pig ears.

We lost it all in mud

And still—We lost it all in mud

We lost it all in mud
We lost   it all in mud

ıud

JOANNA GORDON

ANOTHER TYPE OF AFTER

mountains bleed when

a storm shakes

houses down

our backs

dirt-floods   spitting

jimmy boi's

slippah down

the street

far back and

deep into

the valley

if it continues to rain

we will wake   tomorrow

with mud in our mouths

                    instead of spit

             and still

all we smell is

                                                salt

             rising from

             the concrete

             a thick sigh lying still

                                   through the streets.

JOANNA GORDON

THE EXODUS

Once, a house between two mountains melts,
and liquidates a family fractured over oceans

it happens when the dog dies and then the cat,
dad survives a labor shortage but not without a crooked back.

in a concrete jungle, the milk is imported
your own luck can sweep you out to sea—

in the ocean we have lost a camera, a phone, a slipper,
a watch, a hope, a will, the cost of paradise,

that is really the cost of stolen land, in the exodus
we will leave in droves, cars stacked atop Matson

containers, the salt stuck to our windshields a final
parting gift, if diaspora is a crossing then we find home in

spring, in moss, in the poke shop co-owned by aunties
from home, in Spam grease and seaweed snacks,

in the exodus we leave in droves and ache
for the ocean we turned our backs on. Some of us still visit,

two weeks on the beach each summer, reading
street names aloud but the vowels in our mouths taste

like metal, our skin is now haole-pink,
too burnt for the afternoon sun, we are really

just tourists to this land, and every other,
some of us cling to our state licenses, our bank accounts,

our library cards, some of us are cultural artifacts trying
to remain marked, but what we hold seeps

like water down the lips, melts
like seaweed stuck to the mouth.

SUE PATRICIA HAGLUND

QUARANTINE IN THREE PARTS: MEMORIES DURING QUARANTINE

Part One March Quarantine:
When I Close My Eyes

When I close my eyes I hope to feel
The winds' warm embrace
Silently whispering,
"We are here."

When I close my eyes
I hope to smell
The salty, sweet ocean air
Of waves kissing shorelines
Saying, "We are here."

When I close my eyes
I hope to hear
Beautiful bird songs
Melodically chanting
To the morning dew,
"We are here."

When I close my eyes
I hope to taste
Sky waters,
Bluest, blue drops,

Falling in love,
Falling in light,
Gliding words, "We are here."

When I close my eyes
I hope to touch
The flowering rosy plants
Made of soft petals and prickly thorns
Soundless throbbing veins,
Exhaling, "We are here."

When I close my eyes
I hope to see
Setting Sun
Leaving space
Defining time
For Brother Moon to rise
In opaqueness,
Illuminating paths,
Singing, "We are here."

When I close my eyes
I hope to sense
All my lovely senses
Of Interstitial ways
Navigating through
My eternal being
Remembering,
"We are here."

Part Two April Quarantine:
When I Open My Eyes

When I open my eyes
I hope to see
The words on a page
Flow off my soul
Into my *own* embrace.

When I open my eyes
I hope to feel
The smile on my face
As it falls only to rise
From sadness to joy
From darkness to light
From one end to another
In this small space of mine.

When I open my eyes
I hope to hear
Your guttural laughter
Breaking down the silence
Around
In depth to show
That life is one thing
We hold.

When I open my eyes
I hope to smell
The ethereal fragrances
Of ginger flowers
Permeating

Blooming
Along the mountain edge.

When I open my eyes
I hope to taste
My favorite tea
In company of friends
In an open place
Beyond this current
Confining walls
We call "home."

When I open my eyes
I hope to touch
The salty waters
Washing ashore
Every grain of sand
Only to remind me
A deeper horizon:
Beyond here,
Beyond now.

When I open my eyes
I hope to sense
The beating of my heart
With its rhythmic patterns
As I gaze up in the skies
Lying down in comforting sands.

When I open my eyes
I hope to know
This all soon will arrive.

But for now,
When I open my eyes
All of these appear in my dreams.

Part Three May Quarantine:
When You Close Your Eyes

When you close your eyes
I hope you see light
As bright, shiny gold
As *la cempasuchitl*

When you close your eyes
I hope you hear
Los cantos e instrumentos
Raging through the winds
As the *Café Tacvba* rebel
You are.

When you close your eyes,
I hope you feel,
Brightly, colored threads
Of *P'urhépecha*
Blusa, rebozo
Falda, delantal
Woven stories
Sequin fabrics
Of *Pátzcuaro.*

When you close your eyes
I hope you smell

Fragrance warmth
Of Spring

Durante los momentos
De Tranquilidad.
To balance your thoughts
To plant your roots
In all the spaces
You dance.

When you close eyes,
As the sun sets,
And the moon rises,
May you remember
All of your circles,
All of your brilliance
As the Educated *Chingona*
You are.
Being still and unmoved,
Bravely repeating, *"Fuck It, Not Today."*

AVA FEDOROV

Grateful

2020

Ink, acrylic, watercolor, pastel, and collage on paper

GRATEFUL

I'd like to conclude for you
Illnomadic two
Second Language
My cauldron got that stew
A mix of many places
My trace is very spacious
I had to be courageous walk the path of the ageless.
These sacred
Reflections dimmer off the stainless
When the stain sits
Invisible to digest
Underneath the pressure is where raw beauty manifests
My final fantasy
The contents of my pages
The story of a child who had to wear many faces
The taste is
Bitter but it helped him see the matrix
Every stranger teaching lessons through their fakeness.
Searching for that greatness didn't take it to heart
The art of having patience
I put the horse before the cart
I avoid division listen to my inner vision

Give me light give me breath
I'll give you all of my love
Give me life give me death
Let me work my way up
Give me truth give me honor

I'll make magic with my alchemy
Grateful
For what the universe invest in me

Make decisions based on lessons piling up at intersections with
       intention
I arise find this beat is introspective so
I sat there dissected it found its hidden meaning now the stereo
       projecting it
In rhythm we are meeting of the minds to design purpose
       in soliloquy
A musical communicative line of delivering
This content constructed in the presence of the Koʻolau's cascading
       energy hit you in the poʻo now serenade your cerebellum
       symmetry so obvious that justice and indigenous
       sovereignty is synonymous
It's time for this metropolis to seek to be autonomous no more the
       four four
The corps of the apocalypse
My confidence is through the roof
I'm a survivalist
Illnomadic
Supporter of anonymous
Supporter for the movement to end all politics
Supporter of the people who protect the sacred places.

Give me light give me breath
I'll give you all of my love
Give me life give me death
Let me work my way up
Give me truth give me honor

I'll make magic with my alchemy
Grateful
For what the universe invest in me
I'm grateful
For the time that you spent
Listening to my prose
Hope you caught my intent and I'll close with a last thing that
       needs to be said,
Turn your hewa into pono, make gold from lead, I'm so grateful to
       Hawai'i and Kanaka Maoli
Showing me aloha through the sharing of their stories, teaching me
       a refugee the ways of their ancients, to live aloha 'āina with
       respect for the sacred.

ANN INOSHITA

GO TAKE PIKCHA WIT GRUMPY

My madda said, "You gotta go Disneyland wen you young,"
so me, my sista, madda, and fadda flew to Disneyland.
My parents neva went Disneyland befo, so was good fo everybody.

Me and my sista was in elementary school, so we rode rides like da Dumbo ride,
Alice in Wonderland, Mr. Toad's Wild Ride, and It's a Small World.
We shopped Main Street, and we took pictures wit Mickey
and Minnie.

One day, my madda saw da dwarfs, Happy and Grumpy,
and wanted me and my sista fo take pikcha wit dem.
Happy took pikcha wit us, but Grumpy kept walking.
My madda chased after Grumpy and told him
dat she wanted fo take pikcha wit him and her girls.

I wanted fo tell my madda, no need. Not like he Cinderella
or Snow White.
My madda grabbed Grumpy by his robe and brought him back, so
we can take pikcha.
Grumpy stay looking at da camera wit his hands crossed.

My madda said, "Smile."
We smiled, and she took da pikcha wit her Kodak camera,
and I heard her rewind fo da next shot.

ANN INOSHITA

RED BANANA IN DA FIRST GRADE

My madda wen get red banana
from somebody yestaday,
so I going color my banana red
fo show da teacha dat I smart.

Da teacha wen walk by me fo see how I doing.
I smile showing her my pikcha.
Den she ask me if bananas are red.
I proudly tell her, "Yes."

Her face wen change right dea.
She wen look real mad and tell me,
"Bananas are not red. Bananas are yellow."
I neva know wat fo say.

Afta school, I wen look fo da red banana at home,
but no mo.
Den my madda came home, and I ask her,
"Where da red banana?"

My madda said she wen give um to somebody.
I told her my teacha said no mo red banana
only get yellow kine.

My madda said da red kine fo cooking,
but she neva cook red banana befo.

I look at da empty table and ask my madda again,
"Get red banana, yeah?"

 She wen smile and tell me,
"Of course, get red banana."
Den I show her my pikcha from school,
and she put da pepa on da icebox.

ANN INOSHITA

WE NEVA KNOW WAS GOING BE LAIDIS

Eva since da pandemic, me and my sista go grocery shopping
early in da morning fo avoid da crowds.
Times get one young employee dat spray down da shopping carts
wit disinfectant.
Gotta wear mask and keep 6 feet distance from everybody.
Most people follow da rules, but we get wat we need and go. We no
dilly-dally.

Wen we go Don Quijote, my madda like come wit us
grocery shopping.
We tell her no need come cuz she older and stay in da high
risk group,
but she like choose da groceries and plan wat fo cook.
Hard fo beat my madda's cooking, and she like go.

We go every Tuesday morning cuz get senior discount,
and we wave at da security guard.
Afta we get da groceries, we see da same cashier on da
morning shift.
Good fo see people you know especially during times of COVID-19.

In March, we had da stay-at-home orda cuz had mo COVID-19
infection numbers.
Dat time, was hard fo find rice and toilet pepa.
Lucky ting, my madda always buy in bulk, so we was okay.

Lada on, da government wen slowly open tings up.
Now, it's July, and da grocery stores get mo stuff,
but you neva can tell wen we going have stay-at-home orda
cuz da COVID-19 numbers climbing again.
No mo vaccine, so gotta watch out.

Plenny people still out of work.
Get long line at da food drives.

Lucky ting me and my sista still working.
Lucky ting we can go Times and Don Quijote.
We neva know 2020 was going be laidis.

BRIDGE JUMPING

At fourteen Pueo and Billy turned bridge jumping into a lucrative business. On weekend mornings they rode their mopeds to ʻOheʻo Gulch, arriving before the first wave of tourists came from town.

Those were the days before they were patient with a younger sister, before I witnessed their hustle in person. But in the evenings, when my brother and his best friend returned home, I heard of their triumphs, how much money was made and off whom. All these years later, I can still see Pueo as if he were with me: seated on a bridge handrail, outlined in brilliant blue, calling out to cars who slowed to take in the view.

"Hawaiian cannonball. Five dollas. Ten fo' flip. No coins." He stands and balances, toes wrapping curved metal. Behind him the drop is fifty feet to a pool that looks as if it could fit in the palm of his hand. He dips one foot below the rail, his heel brushing the placard: *No jumping from bridges.*

But bridges are everywhere on this part of Maui, and car-sick children buckled into the backseats of a hundred Mercury Capris. How attractive it is to pull the rental car over, let everyone out. Have they reached the Seven Sacred Pools yet? Is this Hāna? And if so, where are the lei vendors, the cut pineapple, the coconuts waiting to be punctured with straws? The father pulls out the map. The kids, happy to be uncaged, run alongside the two-lane highway. The wife is photographing a yellow crepe ginger. Hāna town is fifteen miles back, and they are well past the land of fruit stands, coconut water, gas stations, and public bathrooms. All that's here is this dark-skin adolescent who possesses neither the jolly quips of yesterday's tour bus driver nor the pressed Aloha shirt of the resort bellhop. Here, at last, is the native in his natural habitat, and he wants $5 for a Hawaiian cannonball.

"What makes it different from an American cannonball?" the father wants to know.

Pueo rubs his nose, the signal for hesitation, and instinctively the father rests his hand over the pocket where his wallet resides. From the other side of the bridge, Billy approaches them, his 'ehu hair golden in the sunlight, freckles bursting prettily across his cheeks, blue eyes bright as the sky. He removes his A's cap from his head and looks over the bridge. "That's not so far," he says.

"Das sixty feet!" Pueo crosses his arms over his bare chest.

"I bet I could do it."

"What, you like jump wit' me?"

Billy sets his A's cap on the ground, beside the foot of the railing.

"Where you from, kid?" the father interrupts.

Billy points at the ball-cap. "Northern Cali." Then, to make sure no tourist mistakes him for a hippie, adds, "Gilroy, to be exact. Garlic capital of the world."

That gets the guy. He laughs, repeats the phrase, "Garlic capital of the world." Maybe he has heard of the town, maybe he hasn't. It doesn't matter. What he sees in Billy—what they all see in Billy—is a true-blood American kid, a memory of himself.

Billy slings his leg over the guardrail. "I'll jump for free!" He has teeth that are mathematical in their evenness, his smile a practice in architectural beauty.

Somewhere, near the end of the bridge, the wife frowns and her husband, without turning, feels her disapproval. "Let's leave that to the locals." He holds one hand out as if to stay Billy while with the other reaches into his pocket. He ponies up a ten, his palm sweaty against Pueo's, and Pueo opens the Velcro pocket of his boardshorts with a satisfying crunch, tucks the bill inside. He climbs back on to the rail, stands with his back to the water, facing the customer. Beyond the bridge, Pueo can see the gentle ascent of the slope toward the rim of Haleakalā. The waterfalls—dozens of them in those days—braid into terraced pools. He smiles. Because his teeth lack Billy's evenness, Pueo, even at his happiest, appears uncertain. He raises his arms above his head and for a second he is suspended—not falling, not jumping, just holding still. He winks at Billy. Then he bends his knees, pushes off the railing, and somersaults to the pool below.

It took two more years before my brother and Billy deemed me old enough to tag along. By then they were sixteen, generous with me in a way I knew they didn't have to be. They had mostly outgrown their old racket—girls and parties and waves worth riding filled their days—but when I was with them we headed out Hāna way. I rode on the back of one of the mopeds, my arms wrapped tightly around a chest newly muscled, and wore the one helmet we owned, its plastic encasement knocking gently against the shoulder blades in front of me. I watched them bridge jump until they made enough money to buy new leashes for their boards or a bag of pakalolo or whatever else they had decided they needed.

Some afternoons we'd ride home and others we'd swim. For my fourteenth birthday, we drove to Waiʻānapanapa State Park to scramble through the lava tubes. We descended into complete darkness, Pueo ahead of me and Billy behind, emerging above a deep pool in an underground cavern. The water was lit from below via a submerged tunnel, and we perched in shadows above it. When I jumped I had the sensation of falling into stardust.

We swam through that underwater tunnel and arrived in a new pool, a new kind of crepuscular silence. Billy's hand grabbed mine and squeezed, as if he were telling me to remember all this, every sensation of it: the textured darkness, the glowing water, the ancient scent of those tubes and caverns. Finally, we swam to a cave that faced daylight and our eyes, accustomed to the dark, ached. We took off running, half-blind, a race up the mountain to where the mopeds waited.

How easily we spent that last day of our happiness. We left Wai'ānapanapa long after the sun had dipped behind Haleakalā, as the eastern sky darkened. I was hungry and damp and tired. On his moped, Pueo took the turns fast, skidding dangerously close to the edge of the sea cliffs. Billy followed, more cautiously, perhaps because I was with him. The air was thick with the scent of rotting liliko'i and strawberry guava, and I buried my face into Billy's neck, knocked that too-big helmet against the brim of his A's cap. I could taste, on his neck, the saltwater from those deep anchialine pools. I leaned my body in tandem with his, pressing into a turn, the moped slowing as we ascended a hill, the engine whirring with the effort to climb, and then we were off again—skimming the edge of the highway while beneath us the ocean appeared feathered and thrumming, like a bird's wing beating against the sky. ❧

JULIET S. KONO

OMITTED

April 24, 2020. DOH is reporting the 13th and 14th deaths associated
with COVID-19 in the state. One is an Oʻahu man who had been
hospitalized since the beginning of April, was over 65 years old, and had
underlying medical conditions. He had a history of travel to Las Vegas
in March.

In its slow approach,
the summer solstice is yet several weeks away,
the number of cases and deaths slowly, surely,
rise like high tide along the North Shore,
yeasty bread on the table,
the mosquito bites on my arm,
their names or faces
we would not recognize or had known
—this, simply sad—
for now, they are known only as numbers,
13th and 14th
in the only likely acknowledgment
that they had lived.

I want to know.
I want to mourn.
I scour the newspapers,
like an old kitchen hand,
for obituaries or mention
of their deaths from COVID,
the valiant fight of warriors they led,
but I find nothing,

as if they had never existed,
their lives,
omitted by illness.

JIM KRAUS

TOPOGRAPHY

The island
is an ancient fish,
a mountain

near the shoreline,
the head of a shark giant,
with lava teeth

and saltwater eyes
who wave-like
circled the oceanic sky

and now
under the waning moon
slowly awakes
to the sea's rising tide.

MOE

My parents' house in Kaūmana slowly transforms into piles of termite droppings, so I carry with me its sounds. My mother's muffled snore from down the hall. The TV in the living room and my dad's laughter to the satire of *Saturday Night Live*. There are the crickets before a silencing rain and the slow leak in the veranda; a tapping cadence against a bag of crushed beer and soda cans— "at least five dollas one bag," Dad would mention. I hear him flick his lighter—once, twice—then drop it on the koa table beside his limu-colored recliner. The ashtray dragging across the leather armrest, two flicks to drop the ashes—one, exhale, two. Coughing. Throat clearing. Mom's snoring fades.

The headlights of a car sweep across the far wall of my bedroom. The neighbors are home from a night at the bar. Dad turns the TV down, leans the recliner forward and peeks below a lowered window shade, metal springs pop and creak under his weight. So nīele. A blade of light cuts out from beneath my mother's bedroom door. Dad kicks back again and changes the channel to National Geographic—*Wicked Tuna*. I slide my feet deeper into the quilt given to me by my tūtū wahine. I turn off the lamp and watch my mother's footsteps splitting light. I try to remember my dreams.

TO THE MAUNA

"You should have left it in longer," his mother said as Maʻa spread butter over a soft piece of toast. "Not even brown."

Standing on a short wooden stool, she turned away from the kitchen to continue removing the small tacks holding the edges of the hae Hawaiʻi to their living room wall.

Stepping down, she wrapped the hae around her arms. "We need this today."

At that point, Aleʻa saw the tight, curly hair drift past the front picture window. The soft, slow footsteps up the staircase, careful of the slippers and shoes.

"Tūtū Maiko?"

"Oi! Aleʻa? You home?" A fragile knock on the screen door.

Aleʻa pressed the hae Hawaiʻi into an open duffel bag and greeted her Japanese neighbor at the door.

Aleʻa embraced Maiko, touching cheeks and pressing her hands into the center of Maiko's back.

"You going up mountain, ya?" Maiko asked quickly.

"Ya," Aleʻa nodded.

"Come, help me carry. I saw you loading your car. I get something for you."

Maiko led Aleʻa to the brown wooden gate between their homes and into her garage.

Between her blue station wagon and rusted washing machine was a round patio table covered with aluminium pans of food: pork and peas, beef stew, fried noodles, rice, chili, Spam musubi, tightly wrapped laulau. On the floor, in a small cooler, five bags of poi, a large tupperware of lomi salmon, a glass bowl of potato salad, oranges, papayas, bottles of water.

Aleʻa looked at Maiko, confused. With her wide, arching smile, Maiko took Aleʻa's hand, and squeezed firmly. "You give to whoever."

"Aye, Tūtū. Too much!"

When Maiko smiled, her cheeks rose sharply. Aleʻa could only hug her gentle neighbor once more in love.

As they passed Kaūmana caves, Maʻa stood on his knees and looked back at the shimmering pans of food in the rear of the car. "I'm hungry," he said, turning his head to his mother's eyes in the rear-view mirror.

"You better not," Aleʻa laughed.

Maʻa noticed the foil covering the rice had opened. "Eh ma, we need to cover this better," he said.

At the side of the road, Aleʻa opened the rear hatch and pulled the foil to try and protect the uncovered food. The foil tore off in her hands.

"Halala," Ma'a said, giggling.

"Turn around, put your seatbelt on," Ale'a said, staring at him with her 'big eyes.'

Ale'a looked around for something she could use to cover the food.

"Eh, bozo, give me my duffel, by your feet."

As Pu'uhuluhulu came into view, the sunlight drew reflections of the blanketing hae Hawai'i in each of the car's windows. ✺

a lesson in grief

I am on the last row of my birth control pills for the month. You know, the ones that are a different color from the rest. While the first three rows contain round, green pills, the last row contains brown iron pills that allow for a break from the hormones being pumped into one's body every day. Maybe it's the mind playing tricks on my palate, but I can taste the blood every time the tip of my tongue touches the round brown pill. I swallow. As my body prepares itself to shed its uterine walls, I am in immense pain, my breasts tender, my back sore, my appetite inhuman like that of a starving wild cat. I lay in bed squinting my eyes at the sunlight that is much too bright. My head is pounding, the auditory hallucinations obnoxiously loud. The voices in my head call attention to my weight gain. I yell from my bed that it's absolutely water weight. The symptoms of my schizophrenia tend to worsen around my time of the month, the natural process of my reproductive organs becoming more of a curse than a future blessing. There's always that underlying fear, the fear that I'd pass my illness down to our unconceived child. I run my hand down the empty space on our bed. There is an imprint of your head still fresh on the baby blue pillow. In the distance is the sound of a toilet flushing and then a running faucet.

You used to ask me why I never cried, why the only two emotions I felt or showed were excitement or anger. Excitement and anger are the two emotions that drive a person to action, to movement. Sorrow tends to leave an individual stagnant in time, and time was something I no longer had. I'm three years shy of thirty now.

It was the year before I graduated when I first told my mother that I was hearing people through the walls. She didn't believe me at first. To have a mental illness was to be weak-minded. Even after sitting in the room with me when the doctor diagnosed me with schizophrenia, she did not grieve. Just sat on the stool beside me silently glaring at me with her hands wrung together. The doctor said that schizophrenia was a lifelong illness. The anti-psychotics would make the voices sound further away, but they'd always be there like shadows. I cried on the drive back to my parents' place. She told me to be quiet. It was my fault, my life, and I needed to fix this.

Restless, I get up and walk to the kitchen, leaving the pillows unfluffed and the blanket crumpled on the right side of the bed. I open the titanium fridge. Still groggy, my hand searches through the arctic fridge for the handle of the pitcher filled with iced coffee I had brewed the night before. I pour myself a cup in my favorite cat-shaped mug and take a sip. The hazelnut coffee does not bring the usual euphoria and burst of energy. Instead, a shot of pain sears down my spine and into my lower back. My stomach churns and I attempt to curb the pain with a king-sized bar of Dove's dark chocolate. Your voice resounds from behind me as you emerge from the bathroom. "Hey, what are you doing? Are you drinking coffee? You know coffee's not good for you when you're about to start your period. Let me make you some tea." You take my oversized cat-shaped mug, dump the coffee out in the sink, rinse it with water, and place it in the dish rack. I nudge you away. It is uncharacteristic of me to allow another person to take care of me. Agitated at the wasted coffee, I say "I'll do it myself."

"It's okay. I can make it for you." You open the wooden cabinet and pull out a white ceramic teapot with pink cherry blossoms painted over its surface. You fill the pot up with tap water, gently wipe the bottom with a rag and place it on the electric stove. With a smooth turn of the wrist, you slowly raise the heat to medium high.

Somehow, the sentiment inspires fear followed by a tinge of

pain. "I can do it. I'm fine, really."

"Go lie back down." You softly press your warm lips against my forehead. "It's your day off."

"It's just cramps."

You lead me by the hand back into bed and cover my legs with the blanket. I fidget until my feet find their way out. My feet are hot, but I say nothing. The fabric of the navy blue fleece blanket proves to be too hot for a summer's mid-morning. The sky is cloudless, the sun shining its rays high above the ridges of Diamond Head. Its rays are blinding.

There are four holes in the white drywall surrounding the glass windowpane in our room, holes drilled by my father who had installed shower curtains instead of window curtains by mistake. At first, the sight of the crude holes in a once unblemished white wall was unbearable. But over time, the walls evolved to incorporate scuff marks from clumsily trying to move a small couch, a dining table, and even the $300 queen-sized mattress we ordered from Amazon into our tiny unit. As pieces of our individual lives trickled into our humble home, more blemishes and stains appeared on our walls, the chemical smell of fresh paint replaced by Bounce fabric softener and lavender-scented Air Wick air freshener, and sometimes even kimchi whenever we cracked open the large plastic jar of store-bought kimchi.

I tore the curtain down myself one Saturday while you were at work. It was one of your evening shifts at your security job and you wouldn't be home till morning. It started off with the air conditioner whirring through the living room. I was washing the dishes after having scarfed down leftovers when the sound of laughter seeped through the vents of the air conditioner. *She's brain damaged, sick in the head. How can she afford to live in this place? I didn't know people like her were allowed to be out and about. She needs to be institutionalized.* That evening, I was psychic and

had superhuman hearing. *What kind of guy dates a mental case?
There must be something wrong with him too.* It was the curtains.
The curtains acted as a transceiver. The seams stitched into the
curtains were wires carrying the voices and thoughts of people
into my mind. I saw the patterns.

I yanked at the thick, coarse, waterproof fabric until both the
curtains and the curtain rod came down with a crash. It left a dent
on the mahogany vinyl floor. Despite my best effort to tear the
thread to pieces, the voices got louder, the transmissions of people's
thoughts stronger. I went into the bathroom, opened the pink
jewelry box where I kept my razors, and hacked at my wrists until
blood dripped onto the white tile floor. Everything made sense
again. No time wasted crying. Fixated on the pain, the voices grew
soft. I told no one, wore a large sweater to cover the wounds. When
you came home the next morning, I told you that the drywall was
too weak to sustain such a heavy metal pole, that it was just faulty
DIY renovating. You nodded your head in agreement and said you'd
hire someone to install the curtains next time. You were just glad
that I didn't get hurt.

To suffer alone is better than being surrounded by people who
transform your whole existence into a sickness. The last time I
was institutionalized in the psychiatric ward of the hospital, I was
admitted by an ex-boyfriend after a long-winded argument about
his infidelity. He dragged me by the hair and threw me head-
first into his dark green pickup truck. When we arrived, he told
the receptionist in the ER waiting room that I was suicidal. They
believed him over a schizophrenic. He left me not a day later for
a woman four years younger, with a bosom two times larger, and
a waist two sizes smaller. I was put on suicide watch for a week.
The nurses stripped me of my clothes and all my belongings and
locked me in a yellow room with no windows, no furniture, just a
white cot with a sponge mattress barely big enough for my small,

5-foot frame. Above the cot, was a camera with a light that blinked red every few seconds. I was given a thin blanket and a large white table with a cup of orange juice. They told me that I would be safer in the hospital, but the voices got louder, bouncing off the ugly yellow walls, screams echoing from down the hall right outside the bolted door.

If I show you that I am suffering, you will stop loving me. Do you understand?

You kiss me on the cheek and I watch you slowly walk back into the kitchen. The scent of sencha and jasmine begins to make its way into the room making me drowsy. Three minutes later, the microwave dings and you return with a hot wet cloth. You lift the blanket and then my shirt and place the wet cloth underneath my belly button.

"You really don't have to do all this. I'm just having menstrual cramps."

"I just don't like to see you in pain." You remove the wet cloth from my stomach which has already cooled down. Before you leave to microwave the cloth again, I grab your wrist.

"I'm fine, really. Please just relax."

"I am. I just want you to feel better," you say, your voice a pitch higher than usual. Your eyes are wide and fearful like that of a child's. In the sunlight, I can see them glimmering. You quickly turn away and walk back into the kitchen. I hear the faucet running and water splashing against the metal sink. The sound of water bounces off the walls and echoes throughout the apartment unit. Your feet pitter patter against the vinyl floor as your body makes its way back to mine.

"Come here. Just chill," I say, reaching for your hand.

You had always been the more intelligent between us two, both emotionally and rationally. You, with your pointed nose, full lips, and bright hazel eyes that glint with a tinge of red in the sunlight,

remind me of Uriel from the Bible with his tall, majestic frame
and sword made of fire. The protector of our Eden. You're six feet
tall, at least a foot taller than me, yet when you crawl into my arms
and rest your head on my bosom, you feel so small like a child. You
nuzzle your head against my chest and inhale deeply.

"Sometimes," you say, "whenever I'm feeling sick, I look through
Facebook for old videos of my mom just to hear her voice. On my
old phone, I had a voicemail of her telling me how proud she was of
me right before she died. But my phone got stolen."

I don't know how to respond. I never do. I wrap my arms around
your broad shoulders and run my fingers down your protruding
ribs. So bony. My fingers make their way up your arm, engraving
in my memory the shape of your body carefully molded by God
Himself. My hands travel to your face. Wet cheeks. I trace the path
of your tears until I reach the ducts of your eyes and gently swipe
the wet drops away.

There is a moment of silence accentuating the spaces between
our bodies. You had told me once that skin can never truly touch
skin, that touch was just an illusion of the mind, that the electrons
within the atoms that composed every part of who we are, always
repelled. You begin to convulse in my arms, silent sobs. Your
mother had passed away when you were in high school from
cervical cancer, and your father, right before your graduation
from alcoholism. I remember the stories. They play out like a
movie every time you revisit them. "He was trying to get sober
for my graduation," you'd say. "I told him that he couldn't come
if he wasn't sober. He gave a lot of heartache to my mom when
I was growing up because of his alcoholism. Got a little abusive
sometimes too." You spent your high school graduation with your
friends, getting stoned and drunk until you couldn't feel anymore,
believing that to not feel was equivalent to forgetting. But you
told me that the memories never went away and that the pain

eventually returned along with dry-heaving spells and the spins.

From the kitchen, the teapot shrieks and the smell of jasmine permeates throughout the entire apartment unit. You slowly get up to turn off the stove and return a few moments later with my favorite cat mug. It is steaming. Eagerly, I grab the mug with my two hands and blow some of the steam away. The first few sips warm my throbbing back and churning stomach.

You sit on the bed beside me. "I used to make jasmine green tea for my mom when she was sick. She said it always made her feel better. She liked it more on the bitter side. I hope I didn't make it too strong."

"It's perfect."

"I see a dimple peeking out. Is that a smile? The first smile of the day?" You nuzzle your lips into my cheek.

"Stop, you're going to make me spill hot tea all over the bed." But I laugh. Rejuvenated, I get up and gently place the mug on the nightstand beneath my paper lamp and embrace you.

Light seeps away from the windowpane as the sun sets and the room is slowly enveloped by a cool darkness. Our unit is humble. One bedroom, one bath, one small stove and fridge located directly in the living room. But we spent a year together here, trying to transform every nook and cranny into a home with colorful decorations and costumes. There are still lights hung up on the walls surrounding our bed from last Christmas.

On Christmas Eve, we drove to Don Quijote, a Japanese grocery store down the road of our apartment to pick out a small Christmas tree. Every year, people from Helemano Farms set up tents on the parking lot of the grocery store to sell evergreen trees. We picked the smallest, greenest one and eagerly decorated it with hand-made ornaments and lights. We put a crocheted angel at the very top. On Halloween, we dressed up just to pass out candy to all the children in the building. It brought you joy to see them in princess and pumpkin costumes, holding hands with their mothers and singing "Trick or Treat!" We bought the king-sized bars despite my disapproval. "C'mon," you said. "It's just once a year. They won't be eating this much sugar every day." You asked me if I wanted kids someday. I told you that I didn't, that schizophrenia was genetic. It would be selfish to bring a child into this world knowing the potential of passing it down.

"But then what does that mean for you?" you asked.

"What do you mean?"

"Are you telling me that you don't believe that you deserve to exist in this world, that everyone who has schizophrenia doesn't deserve to exist?"

"How can you expect them to survive in a world like this? Life is hard enough as it is. And to have a mother with a mental illness? I would traumatize them."

You picked up a square face towel hung over the bathroom counter, wet it, and started wiping the teal paint off my face. "You know what I think? I think you'd make a great mother. Our kid will learn to love and appreciate all kinds of people. And we'll continue to nurture that as they grow."

We were Jack and Sally that year, do you remember?

On New Year's we visited my parents for the first time. The brief, 20-minute car ride from Kaheka Street to their two-story house at the mouth of Tantalus felt longer than usual. You reached for my hand but I pulled away. We drove past Makiki Park, past the cluster of Christian churches of several denominations, and up the steep road. The landscape suddenly transformed into a sea of green, a jungle. We whipped past vines and low-hanging tree branches, occasionally getting hit by a couple of fallen twigs. "It's going to be okay," you reassured me, reaching for my hand again. I let you hold it. "Your mother just cares about you, Yuna. That's just what moms do. Her rejection of your illness is denial. I'm sure she feels helpless deep down. She just wants you to be happy."

When we arrived, my mother greeted you with a huge smile.

"My son," she pats you on the back. "You still so skinny! Is Yuna feeding you or just stressing you out? Come inside and eat before the food gets cold."

We ate until we were sick. Every time my mother saw an empty plate, she'd refill it with jakkop-bap, a floral wild purple rice full of beans; pa jun, a savory Korean pancake made of scallions and wheat flour; sour, ripened kimchi; and kalbi-jjim, a juicy kalbi stew, her specialty. There was enough mochi soup for seconds, thirds, fourths even. I told you to kindly tell my mother that you're full when you're full or she was just going to keep feeding you, to which you responded, "No, ma'am. I was taught to eat all of what I am given with thanks."

After lunch, I pulled you to the side. "I'll teach you how to bow. You have to do it properly. My dad's kind of a stickler for form."

"Okay."

"You start in standing position. Slowly kneel to the ground and put your two hands on your forehead, palm facing my parents. You have to bow until your hands and head touch the floor. While you're doing that, you say saehae bok mani badeuseyo."

"Say bok man e-e-e . . . can you repeat it?"

"*Saehae bok mani badeuseyo.* It's a phrase we say to wish our elders luck and good health in the new year."

"I think I got it."

We stood in front of my parents, my father sitting cross-legged and stoic, my petite mother, smiling, showing off the crow's feet at the corners of her eyes.

"*Saehae bok mani badeuseyo.*" Perfect pronunciation. Our bodies, as though in synchronization, fell to our knees together. I with my hands to the sides of my skirt, and yours, pressed against your forehead.

The sun has fully set now, the tea cold. Diamond Head is just a shadow, a distant silhouette painted against the bedroom window. I turn on my lamp and pick up my cat mug. The loose leaves have fallen to the bottom of the mug. I gulp down the rest of the tea. Chills run down my spine from the distastefully cold liquid. "Thank you. That was the most amazing tea I ever had."

"Do you still have cramps?"

"No. I feel a whole lot better now." The fear in your hazel eyes melts away. Relieved, you smile.

There is a moment of realization, a break from the self. "I'm sorry." I begin to cry, the knot that had been swelling in my chest for years, slowly unravelling. You had once told me that it takes a village to grieve. Someday, I will learn to not attribute my tears to a sickness, to a trip to the mental hospital. I will learn through the tears, to be strong enough to not react in anger to the voices in my head. Maybe even someday, I will be bold enough to transform my body into a vessel of warmth for your child. You told me that it was okay to feel, that the silent language of tears is another language of love.

"I hope I can someday give you the love you deserve," I whisper.

"You already do." 🐾

CHRISTINA N. LEE

HER MIND IS THE SHORE

You don't have to believe me when I say this
but I've tasted God in sour kimchi,
cold and moist, its red soup over steamed rice
and over-easy eggs, yellow yolk running
and golden-fried pollack.
Specks of chili gently sprinkled
over crunchy cabbage, carrots and radish
vegetables gingerly turned and tumbled
by soft hands, blue streams of veins converging
at the knuckles. I've felt God,
in my grandmother's hands.

할머니, 배 아파.
Her warm hands against my tummy,
she chants
쑥쑥 내려 가라,
쑥쑥 내려 가라.
Smooth, smoothly go down,
Smooth, smoothly go down.
Smoothly
wrist rhythmically
turns in circular
motions against
my bare skin
an incantation,
a gurgle, and then a low rumble.
Pain turns into relief
crinkled nose straightens

face slowly relaxing into peace.
Hush hush,
hush hush.
My baby
sleeps well.

I've heard God in Grandma's songs,
low reverberations of her voice rumbling,
each syllable sung in staccatto
자장 자장
우리 아기
잘도잔다.
Her songs,
once grounding me
in incantations and folk songs
that colored my dreams,
disappearing,
disappearing like
rainbow-colored 떡
and gold bracelets
on a first birthday
like old kimchi boiled with
chicken stock and sardines on the weekends like
the sandy shores of Waikīkī,
each year,
her memory recedes.

I've heard Him in the ocean
as it strikes against the rock wall I run
through the sand, the sinews of each muscle
pulling with every push.
Each passing year the shore recedes,

the sand enveloped by sun-tanned dreams.
I wonder which of these hotels Grandma
worked those 12-hour shifts
picking up sand-covered sheets
from the dirtied carpet of careless feet.

Grandma turns and tumbles the decomposed matter in
the garbage bin,
her hands still searching for the red chili paste in the waste.
Sprawled across the floor, crumpled paper and fruit peels laid out
like crunchy cabbage, carrot and radish.
She turns to me and asks
"Did you eat yet?" not realizing
that she had asked me twice in two minutes.
But still, I hear God in her words,
I feel Him,
in her warm hands.

I tell her
my head hurts
and her warm hands
press against my heart
and she asks me,
"Do you feel it?
두근,
두근,
두근.
You are alive."

LANNING C. LEE

THE PRICE OF FISH

In his previous life, my father ran a long-line
fishing business, here in Honolulu,
his crew all Korean nationals he'd sponsored
to come over
along with their families.

My father, a mega foster-father,
with mega foster-family debt, helping
these men, their wives and children,
cosigning mortgages, car loans, credit card applications,
helping with grocery bills, doctor bills,
electricity, water, and phone bills,
rarely reimbursed, shouldering
the financial burden of so many.

I'm a tourist here, on the fish auction floor in Busan,
listening to the screams in Korean over
the price of fish,
some bids for a special, individual one,
others for batches, all fresh off the boat.
In my previous life I would go with my father
to the pre-dawn fish auctions in Honolulu,
listen to the chorus of cries, the coda a catch
rarely paying what my father and the crew
had hoped for, but most times enough to cover costs.

Here now, in my current life,
listening to these Koreans fight

about the value of fish, in an angry language
I don't know,
I do understand their curse to settle for
the ironic highest-lowest price, and I hear
my father's cries, and here, now, in the middle of Korea,
I feel like I'm back home again.

VANESSA LEE-MILLER

WAILUKU

Wailuku,
the raging kahawai,
the river.
Her kāholo,
Her long sinuous journey
begins,
as a watery,
pencil-thin line,
a mere trickle.
Mauka,
way up high,
looking towards
nā lani,
on Mauna Kea.
Her 'auana
is a graceful journey iho,
downslope,
towards rainy Hilo.
'Ae, Hilo,
i ka ua kanilehua.
As she continues to iho,
journey downslope,
a magical transformation ensues
from her embodiment
of a graceful,
delicate trickle.
She widens,
becoming voluptuous,

she's now a raging beast,
plunging
turbulently
downward,
full of 'ena'ena.
Capable of arbitrarily grasping
in her watery fist,
a young, reckless life
and smuggling it
into one of her
many deep,
cavernous pockets,
in her slimy ana.
She'll stash it there,
it's hers,
until the pale, lifeless form
struggles
through a multitude
of tempestuous undercurrents
to surface
somewhere iho,
downslope.

But,
during the course of her journey,
she leaves a trail
of dazzling performances.
After week
upon week
of infinite drops of rain
from nā lani,
awestruck malihini

call these wonders
Piʻihonua Camp Cascades,
Boiling Pots,
Rainbow Falls.
Old Hawaiʻi calls them
Poakana,
Koakanini,
Peʻepeʻe,
Waiānuenue.
She weaves
ever so gracefully
skirting around sacred,
smooth boulders
leaving her mossy footprints
of slippery limu.

She continues to
ʻauana.
In the wee hours of the morning,
from my Hāmākua-facing bedroom window,
I hear her
raging,
bellowing
sounds.
Drowning out
the lonely,
searching calls
of the small scaly river creatures
of the night.

Searching
in blind rage,

she leaves no boulder,
no jagged rock,
no slimy pebble
unturned.
River Moʻo waits,
watching
her every move,
hearing her belches and snorts and eerie releases.
He, shaking out the raindrops from his mane
of writhing eels,
belts out a wicked laugh
"Get plenny time," he says,
slowly
sharpening
his battle-ready claws
against
the skull boulder.
He waits,
patiently,
for the right
moon.

Oh Wailuku,
you watery,
undulating
wahine aliʻi!

Once a graceful trickle
from nā lani.
You've morphed
into a skull crusher.
You stone carver,

you moʻo slayer,
so bloodthirsty
for the fearless,
sweet-weed-scented
swimmer.
Or was it the claw
of the moʻo
of the rain-drenched cave
of goddess Hina,
that dragged
da young buggah
into the murky depths?

Upon reaching her deep, dark, limu-laden
green mouth,
Makaolanakila.
She forcefully
surrenders
her full, swollen self
plunging
once more
into the wide,
stormy bay.
Both river and sea currents
reluctantly mingle.
She truly is
what Old Hawaiʻi called her,
destructive waters.
Wailuku, the river,
life-giving,
life-grasping,
ruthless kahawai.

R. ZAMORA LINMARK

NATIONAL CRISIS

It's terrifying
this rabidly
spreading giant
panda pandemic
America is now
illiterally infected
education-resistant
ignorance insured
a bug gone viral
menacing
multiplying
hostile takeover
hostaging country
club economy
endangering
CEOs VIPs
commander in chief
pork baron privileges
like a tribe
of pangolinistas
in denial of
impending gloom
despite daily doom
meat market crashes
corpse-to-be corporations
inevitable shutdowns
of stocks and sense
shit of reality

placed under strict
"cornteen"
sometimes hyphenated
"kwarrantine"
or "kurantin"
spelling depending on race
and region.

DARRELL H. Y. LUM

BOY AND UNCLE: LOCKDOWN

—*Boy, what means "lock down?"*

—Supposed to stay home except fo essential tings. Not supposed to go out eat, go beach . . .

—*Jes like jail den.*

—Yeah.

—*But if you in jail, you lock up. And if you foget your keys, you lock out. Why dey no call um lock in, cuz you lock inside? No make sense.*

—Lotta tings no make sense, Uncle.

—*No can go store eh?*

—Only fo food la dat.

—*But las time I went market I see all da people touching da lettuce. So I no buy lettuce. I go buy celery. Get one young lady, dress all nice, fancy shopping bag touch all da celery. Pick up. Put back. Pick up. Put back. I stay waiting my turn. She turn around. No, she change her mind. Pick up. Take one, two stalk celery. She put da rest back. I no buy celery.*

—Why you no go kupuna hour, Uncle. Go early, beat da crowd.

—*You evah been kupuna hour? Only get OLD people ovah dere.*

—Das who kupuna is.

—Yeah but, kupuna go market like dey going sightseeing. Go up and down erry aisle. Stop and read da can corn and reach waay in back fo get da freshest one. I tell you, if da can expire in one year, you no need get da one dat expire in two years. Especially if you going open um tonight! Kupuna hour means dey going take da whole damn hour! Kupuna not going in and out in fifteen minute. Dey buy tree tings and go home. Den dey come back tomorrow fo buy what dey went foget.

—You one kupuna too, Uncle.

—You calling me old? You young boys get um easy. Rice come in small bag, not 50 lb. You know rice used to come in cloth bag?

—Yeah, yeah, you was so poor you had to wear rice bag underwear.

—Not me. I had real BVDs. Maybe not fo erryday . . . but I had underwear.

—Eeew!

—What? Weekend, no need.

—Eeew!

—Let's go get shave ice. Hot today, we go take a ride in da car. Get air condition.

—Nowdays, if you catch ride wit somebody not from your own house, you supposed to ride wit da windows down.

—How come?

—So get fresh air so you no breathe somebody else's air. And no run da air conditioner, blow da germs around.

—Sometimes I ride wit da windows down. When your Auntie sneak

one silent one and no say nutting, I stick my head out da window and howl, "Ah-whoo!"

—Not!

—*True. Boy, mo bettah we jes stay home and breathe our own old stink fut air. Da virus no can survive dat.*

NANEA LUM

MĀNOA, OʻAHU

62″ × 74″

Canvas, earth, stone, and water process, carbon ink, ʻalaea earth
pigment, rabbit skin glue, acrylic medium

Nanea Lum paints as a way to express the world from the
experience of Kānaka in Hawaiʻi. She states: "Painting is my
third language after English and Hawaiian, but it is the one that I
practice at the most." Her process-based practice ranges from kapa
to large-scale oil paintings, and it often presents abstract land,
body, and oceanscapes. To best understand why Nanea is painting
it is important to hear what she has to say, in her own words, in
reference to the place she is deeply connected with and how she
interacts with that place through the art form of painting.

"Mānoa valley in its geographic and biological formation is a home
and birthplace of Hawaiian culture, known through oral histories
as a wahi pana (a living cultural landmark). Mānoa means to be
numerous, intensely dark, and dense. The Mānoa ʻahupuaʻa (land
division) has connection to Waikīkī through the streams that flow
mauka to makai (from mountain to ocean). The wai (fresh water)
that flows from the waterfalls of Nāniuʻapo, Luaʻalaea, Waiakeakua
is the life essential element collected and disbursed by the ʻāina.
My painting process begins with mapping these places. I interact
by my modern means, driving to the back of the valley, to visit
places that have a thousand-year cultural significance. I bring
myself to these waters to find out the reason why I paint; I find the
reasoning why I exist.

"A canvas is the object that is offered to the earth first; this gesture is a means to a communication process. I place it in the ground, in the new moon phase, opening the process, the protocols of ceremony commence until the waning phase of that moon is to begin. The pōhaku of Mānoa found in the stream bed are densely compacted clay rocks. I collect pigments for paint from these rocks. Through interaction and giving shared forms of materials between us (myself and the ʻāina), we are engaging in an extended experience of communication."

WING TEK LUM

THE FIRE

based on the 1900 quarantine for bubonic plague
and subsequent fire in Honolulu Chinatown, as
detailed in James C. Mohr, *Plague and Fire*

The health board condemns the shanties
as someone inside has died from the plague.
Other inhabitants are summarily evicted
gathering whatever they can, but with nowhere to go.

The fire department surrounds the perimeter
poised with their hoses for the start of the burn.
A crowd converges, curious, angry, and resigned,
and worried that they themselves will be next.

The fire is ignited as rehearsed
but unexpected gusts come down from the valley.
Firemen vainly try to contain its spread.
People are stunned, immobile, uncertain about what to do.

Before long, embers billow up, wafted by the wind,
and quickly jump from rooftop to rooftop.
Residents rush to stamp out spot fires
tearing down even their own houses to form firebreaks.

Narrow alleyways turn into gauntlets of flame.
A fireball scours the street, combusting all in its path.
Faces are blistered, hair singed, eyes wide from fear.
Everyone is shouting, drowning out the chaos.

A store selling fireworks for the new year explodes.
A lumberyard blazes on and on and on.
A few run home to retrieve gold or papers.
Most, though, just flee with the clothes on their backs.

Inexorably, the inferno marches toward the wharves.
It melts electric coils and a hastily abandoned fire engine.
Volunteers carry on their backs women with bound feet.
Opium addicts, delirious, are rescued from their den.

Sparks fly into the steeple of the church.
Soon it becomes a furnace consuming its beams.
Unsupported, its bells crash into the sanctuary below.
All of Chinatown hears this dirge.

The refugees try to escape the conflagration
wanting to cross the bridge over the stream.
But quarantine militia, pick handles ready, block their way,
leaving them to huddle in a no man's land to wait.

PRANA JOY MANDOE

FOUR FOR WATER

Hush
the stream tra-la-la-ed past our pipe
             to the end of its bed,
slid over a board set on its edge
             like the lips of a mouth
which sucked up its song
             in the dark
of the mountain's maw

that water
             reappeared in the glimmer
the Big Ditches delivered
             to the green and breezy cane
by the road to school
             where nobody taught
what are these ditches
             who picked and shoveled
      who laid the charges who blasted tunnels
             who stayed who died
who survived this theft —

             ask the archives what was left —

I did not know
             the skin of our mountain
was a sponge,
             a filter, a chant,
or a protest letter to the editor

in a late 19th-century Hawaiian periodical

nor had I seen drips hit
        the dry head of a diversion
engineered to take the flow on a ride
        in an aqueduct hugging the valley's side
delivering water to terraces of taro
        to feed the hands
who'd stacked each stone —

        they returned clean water to its home —

no, my course began
        with an East Maui irrigation dam
that stole the stream
        which ended in a written right
to our inch of pipe
        murmuring hussssshhhhh

the Source
we stepped off Beretania Street into the xeriscape
where seed capsules shone like the neck of a pheasant
                                sipping water

we pushed in the lobby doors
to the Board of Water Supply's fluorescence
        stepped into a tunnel onto a tram
        that s l o w   m o t i o n   r o l l e r c o a s t e d   u s
                        over an escarpment
                        of stones with
                        open pores

to a lake in a rock-bubble where nearshore turquoise
lapped out toward shadows that merged with the cavern's jags
in liquid black that could be stone

              or pool

              or intrusion

and we wondered
how full was the cavern
how low could she flow

        leaving white effluvia on the rocks
        like the crust in a glass that's been

              s h l u r p e d
              with a straw

taking the water out to the city pulsing in fountains
at the state Capitol in the wishing wells the car wash
fundraisers where teens in bikinis shoot soap it has gone
to the Water Park and Ice Palace to the toilets

              flushing in all
              the homes and hotels

but
the whole
Board of Water Supply does not know

        how to fill an aquifer
        although it fills our faucets

because recharging the source is not

              a human process

Big Mama

see the mass of Mauna Kea

she gathers clouds like liquid silk and threads them

through the pores in rocks then pours them into perched ice pools that

glimmer like black mica   she   fills the aquifer   who fills it   Big Mama

our   mountain   fills   our   aquifer

The Groundbreaking

on my way to the summit
I check out my cousin guys' sign
Bulldoze Your Own Temple
and I tell myself, wait

who they telling for bulldoze what

cause up top already get
observatories blocking the starlines
so what other temple they talking about,
one ahu for Our Father or Wells Fargo?

could be they got a point but still yet

no matter what
us blue suits with our batons
gotta clear the road of anyone
without tickets to the groundbreaking

then we march up and I take notice

the homesteady young bloods

I feed in my garage, they the ones
link arms against our police line,
across the access road for the D9s

plus, more worse, who I see front and center

but my daughter, Mary-Alice,
chanting *Kū Ha'aheo* in the protest line —
she couldn't stand on the side
with the peeps who no like get arrested?

she knows I gotta do my job

I gotta follow orders, feed everybody,
pay for the house and the Ford 350,
she get college, I get bills,
and the chief said *make this arrest*

so what I do is

take off my polarized shades
put one loose zip tie round her wrists
and I tell her
no let this stop you, girl

BRANDY NĀLANI McDOUGALL

PUʻULOA

Outside our window:
pregnant sprawl of American
war and selective memory—
protrusion of concrete
roadway, white bar hovering
over the rusted wrecks
of turrets, barnacled oil
bunkers, torpedo blisters.
Lokoamano, drained, filled
to build the naval yard.
Docked battleships in service,
Mokuʻumeʻume enclosed,
metal earth mover claws,
hooks ever ready to ravage
awa ulu under the great
white ball of PACOM.
Sure enough, there are
tourists there, too, snapping
like starved triggerfish.
The white uniformed
naval guides might be
telling them now the *USS
Arizona* was a 608-foot
super-dreadnought
that entombs 942 men.
They might salute
the sunken ship, the dead
soldiers, and ask for

a moment of silence.
They will not say
the ship has been leaking
2 to 9 quarts of oil
every day for the past
75 years. Or that since
WW2 the military has
stored its toxic waste
in the water where
it has leaked into
groundwater wells. Or
that there are 700
documented areas
of contamination. Or
that bunker fuel and
other petroleum waste
have been leaking from
a tank farm into an
underground plume
of 5 million gallons
measuring over 20 acres.
Or that mercury is in
the soil. Or pesticides,
dry cleaning fluids, and
metal residues from
the open burning of
ordnances in the soil.
Or asbestos scrap,
polychlorinated biphenyls,
paints and solvents in
the soil. Or tetrachloroethene
and hydrocarbons in storm

drains. Or that in ʻAiea,
where we are close enough
to hear the 8am "Star-Spangled
Banner" blaring, our people
may be walking, our children
may be playing. We may be
giving birth. We may be
bathing, drinking, we may
be eating, we may be breathing—
without knowing, we may be dying.
They might end the moment of silence
for soldier sacrifice, saluting their flag
over Puʻuloa, monstrous womb.

BRANDY NĀLANI McDOUGALL

ʻĀINA HĀNAU

for Kaikainaliʻi and Kuʻuleihiwahiwa

1.

As it is told
there was darkness,
the deepest blackest
darkness called Pō
turning in her sleep,
knowing what it is
not to breathe,
to verge between
need and climb.
He pō wale kēlā,
He pō wale kēia.

Her sleep was motherly,
thin and uneasy. She
dreamt of flying and falling.
Her turning churned
the dark to heat to light
then to fire. She awoke
and gave birth first
to herself.
He pō wale kēlā,
he pō wale kēia.

The earth and heavens
turned hot and darkened.

Stars erupted on her
skin. Makaliʻi watched
as the walewale flowed
from her and welled
over it all and every
where and when
was breath.
He pō wale kēlā,
he pō wale kēia.

2.

Eia Hawaiʻi, he pae ʻāina, he mau
moku, he mau kānaka, he mau
kānaka nui Hawaiʻi ē. He mau
Hawaiʻi kākou mau a mau.

Like you, these islands were born.
They came from Kāne, from Kū,
from Hina, from Lono, from Kanaloa,
from Haumea, from Papa, from Wākea,
from Hoʻohōkūkalani, from Kaula,
from Lua, from Māui, from Pele, from
the deep darkness of Pō: Hawaiʻi,
Maui, Molokaʻi, Lānaʻi, Oʻahu,
Kauaʻi, Niʻihau, Kahoʻolawe.
They fed on water, salt, and heat,
crawled and then stood up in the light.
They grew tall and wide and turned
and slept and laughed and ate and
fought and shared in black and brown
and green and red. They inhaled earth

and exhaled mountains, beaches, pali
and pōhaku. They inhaled sky, exhaled
the rains, winds, and clouds.

Like you, these islands were born,
and every part of them born. Coral
children, worm children, shelled, fish,
limu, grass, gourd, ocean and forest
children. Children of rock and vine
and shrub and tree, fruit and fur.
Water children of salt and spring.
Insect children. Seeded, propagated,
cormed children. Children who slither,
crawl, cling, and creep, who curl and unfurl,
who hatch, peck, bite, glide, and fly.
Rooting, digging, hill-building
children. Hiding, peeping, nesting
children. Brindled, speckled, tentacled,
shape-shifters. Those with eight legs,
with eight eyes, those with four
and two. Those with fins, with iwi
and without. Tasters who sing
their names, and hearers who
answer or retreat. Children of howl
and screech, of paw and claw,
blind and sighted, tail and tendril,
skin and scale, web and wing,
stemmed, veined, and rooted.
Children o ke au iki a ke au nui.
ʻO nā mea ʻike maka ʻia,
ʻo nā mea ʻike maka ʻole.

Older, wiser children born
breathing long before us. Born
like you. Like these islands.

3.

Born are moʻolelo, seeds
strewn, the finest seeds
of stars in the heavens,
the seeds of gods. Born
from ocean, from spring,
from mountain, from pebble
and shell becoming sand.
Born from storm, from tide,
from crash and foam bubble.
Born from shoot, from leaf,
branch, from every body part,
from beyond the body, from
piko, from ʻaumākua,
from the darkness—born
from huli, from lewa, like you.

E hoʻolohe pono: Every
moʻolelo is huli, every one
lewa between pō and ao,
lani and honua, mauka
and makai in the starred
salivary space, teeth
and tongue unleashed, pressed
through the pulse of clenched
jaw, quivering cheek, they
part pursed lips, voweling every

vestige of throat muscle, of larynx,
of diaphragmed breath, of naʻau:

puka mai ka moʻolelo,
hānau ka moʻolelo,
ua moʻolelo nō.

4.

As it is with moʻolelo,
there are always
many versions

As it is told, Haumea
gives birth to mothers
from every part
of her body

Papahānaumoku
gives birth to islands

Hina gives birth to kapa,
to Māuiakamalo,
and to the reef and fish

Hoʻohōkūkalani
gives birth to kalo
and the stars in his body

Pele gives birth to fire,
smoke and steam, then
to new black land

Hi'iaka gives birth to green,
to kupukupu, hāpu'u, pālai,
ama'u, 'ēkaha, kīlau, ni'ani'au,
pohole, pepe'e, palaho'a.

And there are more
mothers giving birth
to everything you see
and don't see. More
mothers giving birth
to bodies of water, of
words, of darkness, of
movement, of light. More
mothers feeding us safety,
shelter, love, beauty.

More mothers who have
always been from more
mothers. You should know
you have many mothers,
and you will be mothers
to many more.

5.

Another of our mothers
is Kahiki, her womb
a double-hulled wa'a
with thatched sails
like wings. In her, we
ate, slept and breathed
saltwater for months,

read currents of wind,
ocean, let ourselves
curl into waves when
heavy clouds darkened
the sky. All was ocean
and hollow sound on
the entering horizon.

The four stars
of Hānaiakamalama
turned, sank slowly
as Hōkūpaʻa,
ʻIwakeliʻi, Nā Hiku
all floated higher
in the darkness.
Below us, dark wings
glided, filtering for limu.
Above us, moon-fade
flash of white wings
glided, circling for fish.

All we saw then
was Kānehoalani,
his fiery eye opening,
a ring of orange
and streaks of red.
We let the waves
carry us in, let
ourselves spill into
light—our islands
unfurling green.

6.

High in the mountains
in the piko of each
of these islands,
where earth sieves
the sky in the kua hiwi,
the kua mauna, the kua
lono, the kua hea,
the wao kele, the wao
akua, the wao lani,
where the air is
a thick howl and
the gods are seeds
of cold cloud mist
billowing between
short, bent trees

Na wai ka moʻolelo hānau?

Descending to
the wao ʻeiwa,
the wao lipo, the
wao nahele,
the wao lāʻau,
where ʻōhiʻa, koa,
kukui, and ʻaʻaliʻi,
where māmane,
lauaʻe, wiliwili,
and ʻōhelo, where
alaheʻe, ʻūlei,
kauila, and maile,

where the uhiuhi,
kōkiʻo, ʻaiea, and
halapepe arouse
fat clouds with
sweetened wafts,
where the fog lingers
and drips and birds slurp,
their songs seeding
the understory

Na wai ka moʻolelo hānau?

Flowing down
the ridges, over beds
of lipo, mossed
pōhaku, ʻiliʻili,
upwelling cool,
the gushing puna
of underground
arteries, from the
darkened blur of
cloud shadow
to the wao kanaka,
the wao ʻilima, the
wao amaʻu, the kula,
where kalo, ʻuala,
ʻawa, wauke,
ʻulu, and maiʻa
flick and clatter
their leaves, and
tufts of tangled
pili ribs bow to

bury their seeds

Na wai ka moʻolelo hānau?

Flowing still
to the muliwai,
where stream
and tide stir,
swirl, the murky
mouth, soil, salt,
and green gurgle
eddying brown,
mottled where
the seeds of moi,
āholehole and
ʻamaʻama feed,
their dark spines
concealing as
they dive together,
channeling
current

Na wai ka moʻolelo hānau?

7.

kūkulu: to build, as a hale;
a pillar or post, a horizon;
to erect; to raise, as the frame
of a hale; to bind together, tether;
to stand in unity; point where
the sky meets the horizon; border
or edge of a country; Kūkulu
i ka ʻōlelo. Kūkulu hale. Hāpai
i ke aloha ʻāina o Hawaiʻi
i nā kūkulu o ka honua.

hāpai: to be pregnant;
to conceive; to give possibility;
Adj. also to have conceived;
to carry, to honor, to raise up;
to kākoʻo, as another's testimony
or endeavor; to offer praise;
to begin, as a speech or journey;
Hāpai pū. Hāpai i ka leo.

papa: mother of the islands;
having a flat, smooth surface,
as a soft stone or a wooden board;
a native born in a place; a story
in a building (papa lalo, the lower
stories; papa waena, the middle
stories; papa luna, the upper
stories); to prohibit or rebuke;
to place closely together as of a
thicket of plants; in unison, all
together; a distant ancestor; a
race; a family

makuahine: a mother;
aunt or female relative
of the parents' generation;
Lit., female parent; makua:
a provider, a mature person;
to sustain and make strong;
full grown; hoʻomakuahine:
to act as a makuahine
or to treat as a makuahine;
ʻO Hawaiʻi kuʻu makuahine.

pou: a post, pillar, or shaft; the ridge, as of a nose; the mast of a canoe; **pouhana**: working posts; the two end posts of a hale, the tallest posts, their length establishing the hale's height; **pouomanu**: post of the bird; the center post of a hale; **pou kaha** or **kihi**: the corner wall posts; **pou kukuna**: the end wall posts; gate, door, or gable posts

pūʻao: the os tincae, opening of the uterus, the orifice of the womb; place in shallow water where a retreating wave meets one coming in; **pū**: conch shell, tree, the head of the octopus, canoe end piece, a coil of hair, to unite, to be together, entirely, completely; **ʻao**: a new shoot, leaf, or bud, especially of kalo

wahi ʻoiʻoi: a tenon fashioned at the upper back end of each pou; **wahi**: a place, position, site, setting; **ʻoiʻoi**: full of sharp points, sharp; to protrude or jut out; also called the ʻule

uli: earliest stage in the development of a fetus when the child's body first begins to form; the blue sky; a dark color—black, blue or green, including the deepest blue of the sea, the thick green of the forest, and black clouds; to guide a canoe; to gurgle like water beginning to flow

auwae (also auae): the chin;
Adj. expert; a curved
notch cut on a pou to form
a chin below the base
of the wahi ʻoiʻoi; used
to connect the pou to oʻa;
also called the kohe

mana (also kaha): stage in the
development of a fetus when
the child's limbs begin to grow;
stage in the growth of fish
when colors first appear; power,
glory, authority, charisma;
a branch or limb of a tree
or a human; to branch out and
be many; the food chewed
by a mother and fed to her baby

kaupoku (also kaupaku):
the upper ridgepole of a hale;
the highest point, the roof,
the ceiling; to erect the upper
ridgepole so as to divide the
living area of the hale from
the bonnet or cap of the hale;
to thatch the ridge; a partition;
Fig. the greatest

kuamoʻo: the spine,
the backbone of a human
and non-human relatives;
a road or familiar path;
the bottom of a canoe; a near
and trusted relative of an aliʻi
who attended to his/her/their
needs and possessions; ʻohana

**kuhikuhi puʻuone (also
kuenehale):** a seer; a class
of kahuna who advised
on the location and building
of heiau, hale, loko iʻa, and other
important structures; an architect
and architectural engineer
Lit. to direct mounds of sand

pale keiki: to deliver
a child; an obstetrician;
a midwife; class of kahuna
who advised families and
women throughout pregnancy
and before and after childbirth.
Lit. to shield the child

o'a: the rafter of a hale, the beams of a roof; timbers in a ship's side; sides of a rock wall, the gills of a fish; the mouth of an eel; the musical staff, the five parallel lines on which music is written

kua'iole: the topmost ridgepole of a hale securing the ends of the o'a to the kauhuhu; kua: the back, windward; to carry on the back, as a child; to hew, chop, chip, cut out; to fell, strike down; block of wood on which kapa is beaten; women's hale used for making kapa; Ma ke alo o kēia aina, he kua o ka moku ia; 'iole: mouse or rat

kauhuhu: the ridge or edge of a precipice; the lower ridgepole lying beneath the kua'iole and running the length of a hale to which the tops of the o'a are secured

alawela: a dark line that grows from the top of the abdomen and from the bottom of the abdomen of a pregnant woman; when the lines meet in the navel to form one line, the baby would be born *Lit.* the warm pathway

pohā ka nalu: breaking of the waters in labor; pohā: to burst forth suddenly, to thunder; to rush upon; to flow out; *Adj.* cracking open; light sparkling; nalu: amniotic fluid; a wave, the surf; to be full of waves; to make waves; to be in doubt or suspense; to wonder at; to speak to one's self; to think to one's self; to search for truth

nahunahu: to feel the first pains of childbirth; a biting and sharp pain; to bite often

kaola: beams laid
across the rafters
of a hale used
to strengthen
the structure

hāhā: to feel the body
with the hands so as
to diagnose sickness or
to turn or reposition
a baby in the womb into
the position for childbirth
(done by the pale keiki)

kanaka kūkulu hale: builder
of a house; construction worker

koʻo kua: helper for the pale keiki
who sits behind the woman in
labor giving back support, and
with arms wrapped tightly, pressing
down on the mother while she is
bearing down

ʻaho: a purlin of a house; breath,
to breathe; **ʻahopiʻo:** thatch
support purlin to which layers
of pili would be tied; **ʻahokele:**
horizontal purlin; **ʻahopiʻokuahui:**
purlin support rod; **ʻahopueo**
or **keʻa:** fixed purlin, main purlin

kōhi: to be in labor and endure
the pains of childbirth; to gather,
as fruit; to separate, as a kalo
from the huli; to dig a hole;
Adj. fat and rich, as food; prolonged

holo: the diagonal strut
attached to the inner side
of the roof frame and extending
from the upper end of an oʻa
at one corner to the lower end
of the oʻa at the other corner;
to run, sail, ride, go; to flow,
as water; *Adj.* determined,
agreed upon, settled

ʻinaʻina: the reddish discharge
preceding labor in childbirth;
the mucus plug or bloody show.
"Ua hemo ka ʻinaʻina o ke keiki,
ua kokoke paha i ka manawa
e hānau ai" (Pukui & Elbert)

pueo: hale lashing;
the Hawaiian owl;
"Kuʻu manu noho pū
me ke kanaka" (Pukui &
Elbert), a riddle punning
ʻaho pueo and pueo
for the hale

halakeʻa: upright posts within
the hale to which the laʻaukea,
or cross ties, were fastened

pili (also lule): a long coarse grass
used to thatch hale, so called for
how pili seeds detach from
the stalk and stick to a person's
clothes; preferred over other
grasses for its fragrance and
symbolism; shingles, so called
because they replaced pili on
the roofs of hale; to cling or stick
to, to be with, to belong; to agree

kahi hāiki: the birth
canal; a narrow place;
"Aia nō i kahi hāiki,"
said of a child about
to be born (Pukui &
Elbert); hā: to breathe
through the nostrils;
iki: small

hōʻiʻī: to strain, moan,
and grunt, as during childbirth
and while enduring labor pains

hauʻoki: medicine made of hau bark
and given to women in labor to ease
pain and to help create walewale
so the baby can slide out more easily;
hau and ʻilima blossoms may also
used; hau: tree with heart-shaped
leaves and flowers with five large
petals that change through the day
from yellow to dull red; a kinolau
of Haumea; ʻoki: to sever or separate

lohelau: the wall plate
of a hale frame on which
the oʻa were fastened;
Adj. exhausted, as a human
due to fasting, hunger,
or fatigue; excellent;
lohe: to hear, to obey; lau:
to spread out broadly, as a leaf;
the leaf of a tree or face
of a person; the number 400;
to be numerous or many;
Aia lau kanaka ai e aloha ʻāina ai.

kuakoko: pain or distress, as of
a woman in childbirth in bearing
down labor; *Adj.* Of or belonging
to childbirth; kua: The back
of a person or animal; the top
of a ridge or high land; the front
side of a place; koko: blood;
to squeeze or press; to pull this
way and that; to fill or fulfill;
the braided strings used to carry
calabashes; a natural phenomenon
of falling rain where sunlight shines
through and it appears reddish

8.

Before first is cloud
edge thirst, is electric
current slither. Before
first thrums illiterate
in lethargic bloat.
But before first was
just fine to thirst,
slither, thrum, bloat
in darkness, to wait
to become—and well,
before first was
still *technically* first—
which is to tell you
you have to be
careful with firsts
since first is one
of many mothers
without memory of
the firsts before her.

What I mean
is there can be
more than one first:
It is true that Pō
was first, that first
was slime, the plant
people, the ocean
people, first, that
four, six, eight,
and more legged

people were first.
It is true Laʻilaʻi
was the first woman,
who brought forth
the ao with Kiʻi,
the first māhū
and Kāne, the first
man. From them,
Kamahaʻina was
the first child. It is
also true that Papa
was the first woman,
who birthed the islands,
and Wākea, the first
man. It is true Hāloa
was the first child, but
stillborn and buried,
that from his grave,
the first kalo sprouted,
its leaves tall, stalks
trembling, its iʻo
momona enough
to feed all the firsts
to come afterward.

What I mean
is we can never
really know enough
so you have to be
careful with firsts.
ʻO ke akua ke komo
ʻAʻoe komo kanaka.

We are all always
firsts and before
firsts becoming,
bursting in form,
in new possibility.

9.

With you
my body was Pō,
some unknowable
dark dwelling full
and slow. The world
was water to you.
I hope it was heart
beat and song, too.

When you were
wing flutter I slept
long and had dreams
of flying and falling
from where toward
where I don't know.

When you were
heleuma turning
and sinking, my body
swelled and flooded.
Sleep was in waves.
I dreamed of my
father who loved
the ocean and woke

in sweat. On my skin,
silver rivulets zigzagged
like lightning from
my piko. A dark line
trickled down from
my heart and up from
beneath my belly, over
the whole of you,
the whole of me.

The world was water.
And heartbeat and
song. I was an opening
nuku, almost high
tide, a heavy heap
of cloud, full and still
somehow floating.

10.

Now I can
only tell you
what little I know
about darkness
about islands
about mothers
about water
about birth

I can tell you
that when the time
came I did not need

to know about any
of it I just had to
let my body be
darkness
islands
mothers
water
to birth

I had to move
toward darkness
I had to breathe islands
I had to rise mothers I had to
fall water I had to turn dark I had
to float islands I had mothers to breathe
water darkly I had to sink islands I had mothers
to lose water my body darker I had islands to breathe
mothers I had water to find darkening my body islands I
had to inhale mothers I had water to exhale darkness I had
island mothers to feel water I had dark island mothers to become
me I had water to darken islands to inhale mothers I had water
dark islands to exhale mothers I had water to forget darker me
I had islands to mother remember you I had to open water
open darken islands to inhale mothers I had watered dark
islands to exhale mothers I had to open water to rise
darkened island mothers to open watered darkness
I had islands to open to fall mothers I had water
to let dark island mother water make me
darkness islands mothers water
strong inhale darkness so
islands exhale mothers so
water I had dark to open islands

mothers to open darkness to be stronger
than I knew islands mothers water I could ever
be I had to push with darkness islands mothers water
push so I could be darkness islands mothers water for you push so
all darkness for you all islands push for you so all mothers for you
push all water for you all for you all light for you for us to breathe.

11.

After it all, you came
into light, eyes open.
Your father caught you.
Your throat cleared,
you breathed. your
father brought you to
my breast, you were
warmed, fed. You slept.

For you, kuʻu maka,
I floated full with thoughts
of who you would be.
Stars spilled premonitions
of your face, your voice.
But you have to be
careful with firsts, and so
I had been studying and
steadying, trying to
choose what was best,
what may have been
more like our kūpuna,
what natural birth books
and videos said could give

you optimal health, a less
traumatic birth. I had a doctor
who said I was *unfortunately*
geriatric, tracked my weight,
had me drink orange sugar
syrup to measure my insulin
response. Another doctor
screened for genetic diseases,
urged me to let them stab
a long needle in my womb
to screen for Down's syndrome.
Another who said I may have
cervical cancer and wanted
to cut part of my cervix
though it could hurt you.
I was told over and over
that my body was failing,
that I could be dying, that
I may be hurting you, that
you may be hurting me.
I hated them. I cried.
All the times I was so
sick as a child, struggling to
breathe, on IVs, stuck with
needles—my body exhausted
and at the mercy of men
in white coats or blue
scrubs, when one was able
to get me alone—it all came
back. I was older and stronger,
but afraid of being in a hospital
again, of needing to stop

someone, and being unable,
again, for both of us.

I was lost. I had long talks
with you. I sang to you.
I sang for you. I asked
our kūpuna, your grandfather
for help. I found a doula,
then a midwife to help me.
I found home birth. I found
a birth class for Kanaka
women. I found Haumea,
I found Papa, I found Pō.
I found ʻāina, I found aloha.
I sang to you. I sang for you.

And I found, when you
were born, our bodies were
strong—we were always
enough. Your breath
to my breast, we fed
and breathed together,
slept safe at home.

12.

I'm not sure where I first heard that Kanaka women
do not scream when they hānau, that doing so would
be considered embarrassing or attention-seeking.
I've never seen another Kanaka woman hānau, not
even your aunties, and it never seemed appropriate
to ask. I can tell you, though, that when the time came

I didn't scream—not because I was worried I wouldn't
be Kanaka enough if I did, or that somehow I'd bring
shame to my ʻohana (those kinds of self-conscious
thoughts don't really happen since your focus isn't
on what others might think of you)—but because
screaming seemed so loud and outward, when all I
wanted was to go inward. When you hānau, you stay
with your body, pulsing through every contraction, but
in the soft lull between the rise and fall of waves you find
hānau makes time stretch slippery tentacles to hold you
as you slide between pō and ao, not quite dreaming.

13.

You were in the dark waves
for a time, your body a pearl
of flesh, hands and feet formed,
ears, nasal passages, a tongue
and palate in your mouth.
Something in the dark called
and you followed, leaving
only your body to come
into light. You were wrapped
and held before you were buried.
You are loved and missed.

In this time, when your child
dies in your womb before birth
an American medical doctor
will do an ultrasound. As you watch
the tiny blurred body on the screen
he'll tell you the fetus is no longer

viable, that you must decide—
D&C (dilation and curettage)
or wait to miscarry at home.
He will explain D&C involves
dilating your cervix and then
scraping and suctioning the fetus
and placental tissues out of you.
He will say that if you wait
for your body to miscarry, it could
take weeks and will be painful
and messy. You feel very alone.
You think of all the ways you
caused this, how your body—how
you failed because *you* mis-carried.
You try not to tell anyone
because you don't want them
to say it was probably for the
best or at least you weren't
that far along or that you need
to just let it go. In another time,
you would have had ʻohana
around you who knew what to say
and do to help you. A Hawaiian
medical doctor would hāhā
your ʻōpū as you described what
happened and told you *he keiki*
heʻe wale or he keiki hāʻule wale,
a child who has flowed away,
a child who has fallen like rain.
You would be given tea to drink
and time to grieve, pray, reflect,
and dream, and you and your ʻohana

would be asked to share feelings
to heal you, and when it was time
for your keiki to flow from your body,
your keiki would be wrapped in kapa
and planted as songs fell like rain.

We tried our best to give that to you,
ku'u keiki aloha. You sank down from us
like water, our love for you loosening
the earth beneath the laua'e, its cradling roots.

14.

puka: a doorway, an entrance
to a hale; the main door to a hale
was in the middle of the front,
a smaller door at the rear; any
place of entrance; to pass
through or emerge from
a hole, crevice, or doorway;
to rise, as the sun or as
a subject to overthrow
the authority of a ruler;
to move from one state
or condition to another,
as from ignorance to
knowledge, as from keiki
to makua

hānau: childbirth; to bring
forth, as a mother (applied
to animal, rock, and human
peoples); to come from but
be separated, as a hua
from the moa or as kowaū
from iʻa; to be born; *Adj.*
having the ability to bring
forth as a mother, as ʻiliʻili
hānau, birthing pebbles, or
as ʻāina hānau, birthing lands

ʻukiʻuki: the Hawaiian lily,
with a short stem and long,
narrow leaves, from which
arises a cluster of white or blue
flowers; its leaves were dried and
braided into cordage to paehiʻa,
to tie on thatch for a hale

ʻukiʻuki: the Hawaiian lily
producing blue berries, which are
boiled and used to make a grayish
blue dye for kapa; a kapa used
to catch a baby who was just
born was dyed with ʻukiʻuki

kala: the gables or ends
of a hale, in distinction
from the sides; to absolve;
Adv. spoken of time, but
used only in the negative
'a'ole, as, 'a'ole e kala
ke kūkulu ana o ka hale
lāhui Hawai'i ma'anei

'ale'o: a place sometimes
built in the upper part
of the hale, a kind of attic
used as a lookout or
to store family treasures;
Adj. high above

kū'ono: the part of a hale
opposite to the door
on the inside; a corner
of a room or a hale (kihi
refers to corners on
the outside); a bay, creek,
or a gulf, where the ocean
forms an inlet on the land
(see kaikū'ono); 'A'ohe
mea koe ma kū'ono.

ēwe: the navel string;
ancestry; ancestral descent;
the place of one's birth and
where his/her/their kūpuna
were born; special care must
be taken to bury the ēwe
of a child in his/her/their
'āina hānau; 'Ō kākou nō
nā ēwe hānau o ka 'āina. Eia
ke ēwe 'āina o nā kūpuna.

'iewe: the placenta
through which an infant
was fed while in his/her/their
mother's womb; the afterbirth;
an infant just born; special
care must be taken to bury
the 'iewe of a child
in his/her/their 'āina hānau

kilo: to look earnestly;
to study intensely, as
the stars or the clouds
or the ocean or a child;
to foretell the weather
or the future; to look
for signs; a judge;
a prophet; a kind
of mirror; to glean

piko: long thatch of pili hung
to cover the door of a new hale
that was ready for habitation.
The thatch was cut by a kahuna
in a ceremony to ʻoki ana i ka piko
o ka hale, as one would do with
a newly born baby; the summit
or top of a mountain; the end of
a rope; a corner or boundary of land

piko (also hāwele): the navel
and the umbilical cord; *Fig.*
blood relative or the genitals;
the crown of the head;
the center; wauke rootlets
from a mature plant ready
for replanting; where a stem
meets the leaf, as of kalo;
special care must be taken
to bury the piko of a child
in his/her/their ʻāina hānau

niʻo (also paepae puka):
the doorway or threshold
of a hale, considered
very sacred; to sit in
the doorway with the door
open; to lean over and sleep

pueo: the Hawaiian owl;
an ʻaumakua to some ʻohana;
He manu lele hihiu; to rock
back and forth while holding
an infant; He keiki a ka pueo, said
of a child whose makuakāne is
unknown

kuwā: a prayer given to
consecrate the completion
of a new waʻa, ʻupena, or hale;
offered during the cutting
of the piko of the hale

māwaewae: the path clearing
ceremony celebrating the birth
of the hiapo, to dedicate the child
to the ʻāumākua and to bless all
siblings to follow from the
makuahine

hale: a house, a dwelling place;
'ohana had 6 or more hale:
a heiau for worship; a mua
for men's eating; a noa, where
all of the 'ohana could be
together freely; an aina
for women's eating; a kua,
where women beat kapa; and
a pe'a for women during
menstruation and childbirth.
A separate hale moe could
also be included for the 'ohana
to sleep in, though without one,
an 'ohana slept in the hale noa.

keiki: little one, a child,
no matter which gender;
offspring, whether a child
or grown person; a descendant
of any number of degrees;
the young of animals or plants,
such as an offshoot of kalo
or kī; 'O kākou nō nā keiki
hānau o ka 'āina makuahine.

15.

After it all, you came
into light, eyes open.
Your throat cleared,
you breathed. You
were brought to my
breast, you were
warmed, you fed,
squeezed my finger.
Your father cut
your piko. You slept.

For you, ku'u hi'ilei,
I knew more, but each birth
is different. I was careful

with you, guarded. I miscarried
at 11 weeks the year before.
We were 14 weeks along
before I told anyone except
your father about you, but
I talked to you, sang to you,
asked you to be strong. I studied
and steadied, like with sister,
I rubbed my ʻōpū with kukui oil,
went for walks. I tracked my own
glucose, ate poi, limu, lūʻau, eggs
and fish, refused the orange sugar
syrup, recorded everything I ate.
When the doctor and nurse said
no one has ever refused, I fed them
logs and charts, said they could
label me overweight and diabetic,
but I would not drink it. They left it
up to other doctors, who I also fed
logs and charts, and who, after
several weeks, were finally full.
It was a small victory, if you can
even call it that, but it was
the first time I felt my decisions
for our bodies were respected.

Like before with your sister,
it was all so patriarchal and
colonial. I wanted to be closer
to our kūpunahine, so I learned
how to kuku kapa from Aunty L.
I bought a kua, hohoa, and

iʻe kuku from Aunty D. One
of my haumana, Aunty A,
joined us to learn, too. We
three Kanaka women went
to the wauke, with permission
from Aunty M and Uncle K,
offering our oli to Mānoa
and Kāneʻohe. We stripped
the stalks and soaked the white
inner bark. After a week, we
met again, sang our oli to
Kānehoalani, then began,
our voices quiet, as the music
ʻouʻou, ʻouʻou, ʻouʻou, ʻouʻou,
wood against raw cloth, water
and wood echoed, until white
sheets of kapa flowed out,
wet and thin, and our arms
and shoulders ached. You
were there, sloshing waves
inside me. A few weeks later,
when I was nearly 36 weeks,
my water leaked. Grandma
stayed with sister, and we went
to the hospital where we were
told we needed to induce labor
early. The doctors and nurses
inserted IVs in me, taped sensors
to my ʻōpū to hear your heartbeat
and to monitor my vitals. Your
father and I went over our birth
plan. They started the pitocin,

and I repeated that I did not
want an epidural. I tried not
to be afraid of you being early,
of feeling everything more
intensely. Your father and I were
mostly alone counting between
contractions, waiting. I told him
to remind me that each time
was only going to be a minute
and that each time would bring
me closer to you. Just before
the last contraction, I felt you
drop down inside me. There were
other rooms with other women
in labor and so the nurse had told
me not to push, but my body
and you took over. Your father
screamed for the doctor, who came
but had only seconds to put
on his mask and gloves before
you were born in one big gush.

16.

E kuʻu mau ʻōmaka i ke kīhāpai:
may you always know these islands,
like you, daughters, are more
than enough, know that like you,
they are everything beautiful,
everything buoyant. Their winds
and rains and mountains, ravines
and valleys love without question.

Like our islands, may you give birth
first to yourselves then love always
with green tenderness, thrusting
your hands into mud, opening
your body into ocean, knowing
these islands are here for you,
for your children and their children,
knowing we are these islands.

For you, may there always be refuge,
safety within the walls you reach,
behind borders, under flags, and in
your own bodies. May you always
be grateful for peace, for open harbors
not freely entered, for treaties honored,
for nothing taken that was not first
given, for iwi still earthed, for new
coral growth unbleached, for black
cloud cover and trees, breathable air,
a beach, stream, or ocean without
plastic tangle or sewage or toxic seep.

I wish you words and medicines
that lift and heal, vegetables and fruit
from organic earth, free flowing waters
from mountain to ocean, daughters, cool
and clean, unowned, shared. I wish you
ocean-salted rocks and shells you can taste
and hold in your mouth, blades of grass
and ridged bark—all coolness and warmth
to press to your cheek, to your lips. May you
know love in every form, but always

in the food you eat, that you love the crust
dried poi makes on the skin around your lips,
the dark green of lūʻau, soft steam of ʻulu,
of ʻuala, the way you must slurp the red wild
of ʻōhiʻa ʻai—all from ʻāina you've curled
your toes into—may you always be full.

May there be hiding places to keep you
as hidden as you want, climbing places
to keep you above, flying places, resting
places, low-lying and high cliff caves,
more places carved by winds and rains,
salt and waves, fragrant jungles, terraced
gardens, islands old and still being born,
places where you wait for welcome,
places that you know are not for you
or anyone to enter—may you protect all
of those places and may they protect you.

May the wind and waves lift you up
and may you let yourself fly, wonder,
from a pali overlook as ʻiwa or pūʻeo
circle above, or as koholā or naiʻa
breach ocean in the distance,
about lightness and sky—that you
remember you can rise high above
whatever may hold you down.

May you hear these islands breathe
with you, let them be big enough
to carry you, small enough to carry
with you. May you know these islands

depend on your breath, that the ocean,
rains, and winds need your voice.
That every green growing thing lives
and births more green growing.
That there is safety and warmth
enough, shade enough when you
need it—water, food, shelter, love.
That you sleep deeply and
let yourself hear our kūpuna.

May you know smallness—know
to be careful and think of unseen
workings, to remember the smallest
can be the strongest, to feel you are
islands like ours, not separated
by ocean—but threaded—your roots
woven and fed by the same fire
and water and salt and darkness.

May you know immensity, too—
that even when you think you are
alone, that you feel the ocean
in your sweat and tears, that you
watch rain wash the hillsides
into a dark stream and see your skin,
that the sun, moon and stars, dark
underwater caverns, underground rivers,
all you see and don't see of 'āina,
are your kūpuna, your 'ohana in
your every breath, that something
of you, something of all of us before,
and something of all of us to come

are these islands. May this always
be with you: E ola mau, e ola nō.

Note from the Author

This poem reflects on what it means to have an 'āina hānau, a birth land from
which we are genealogically connected, as well as what it means to *be* an 'āina
hānau, as all mothers are for their children. To ho'omakuahine, to act as or to
be treated as a mother, is a tremendous honor and kuleana. I wrote this poem
as part of my own continuing huaka'i as a makuahine living in this time when
'Ōiwi birth practices and approaches to caring for and raising children continue
to be repressed. Part of the kuleana of having keiki has meant that I need to
do whatever I can to learn 'ike Hawai'i and in turn teach my keiki. Sections 7
and 14 of this poem, which are composed entirely of dictionary entries, most
clearly demonstrate that learning process. In those sections, I drew definitions/
translations primarily from the Hawaiian dictionaries written by Lorrin
Andrews (1865) and Mary Kawena Pukui and Samuel Elbert (1986), but I also
consulted Mary Kawena Pukui's *Nānā i ke Kumu* series and other books and
essays, and David Malo's *Mo'olelo Hawai'i*. I learned so much from being in Kōkua
Kalihi Valley's Birthing a Nation program. I am especially grateful for Pukui's
contributions, as she trained as a ko'o kua in her younger days and could speak
intimately to the knowledge of pale keiki, to which we must now reconnect.

JONATHON MEDEIROS

QUARANTINE POEMS: MARCH 20–JUNE 21, 2020

March 20, 2020

This spring break, though spring is a day early across the country,
Has been paused by a virus.
That other spring break, five years ago, was extended because
I needed to finish the floor and the plumbing.
We couldn't stay in that match box beneath Mike and Kat much
        longer,
The four of us in one room.

There were so many trees there, spilling over everything,
The rock walls dripped with ferns, moss, littered with wilting
        flowers from the banana,
The hibiscus, the bougainvillea.
The vanilla vines and staghorn threatened to completely engulf
        the guava,
Behind a wall of all the greens the world has seen,
And the scent of cookies.

When the doors finally worked, and the toilet flushed, and the sink
        drained,
We made our way, our little family, too big for the studio on Līhau,
Behind Mike and Kat's garage, beneath their bed,
We made our way to that little hill above the sea,
And we made a home out of that house.

That spring break five years ago, the yard was bare,
Flat, not a plant in it, except for the overwhelming tangle of aloe.
But now I sit here, in this spring on pause, surrounded by my family,
By the signs of having lived, of living still, luckier than Kat and Lau.
I sit on the deck that wasn't here, looking at the sea that always is,
The breeze cooling me, bringing the honeysuckle to my nose,
Bird song to my ear.
Every plant we've put in the ground rustles, bends, dances,
Leaves and blossoms and fruit (the outcome of labor) each waving
        to us, to each other,
And what of the roots that grow below the once bare yard?
That world is an unknowable place now, more complicated than the
        sky, I think.

And I sit on the deck
That wasn't here,
With my partner that is,
The girls drawing, writing, squabbling, asking questions, waving
        to each other and us
And I know
That this world is an unknowable place, more complicated than
        the sky.

March 21, 2020

Makaleha is clear today, unobscured, but dull
In this mid-morning light of my first bike ride during quarantine.
The countless waterfalls visible just days ago
Have receded, leaving gray or red or umber scars.
These too will vanish in a matter of days, replaced by the growing,
Living green of the jungle that clings somehow even to sheer,

vertical cliff.
As the road curves and dives down to the first bridge
I always have a thought, "I knew someone in that house,"
And I struggle to remember who they were, why *Alien* on Betamax
Made its way from that house to ours, like an egg in a box,
And I struggle to conceive of why I watched that movie, alone,
Home from school one day . . . was I 8? 10? Too young, probably.
And I remember the scene at the end, Ripley in her underwear,
And the family friendly movie in the same box of Betamax tapes
(*Around the World in 80 Days? It's a Mad, Mad, Mad, Mad World?*)
With the 70s porn dubbed over the title sequence, 3 or 4 seconds
Of contextless sex.

And that thought, series of thoughts,
Is instantaneous, self-contained,
And it doesn't move with me
As I take the curving hill down and away.
It stays there, on the side of the road, under the trees, near
        a stream,
Near a group of adults around a fire, mosquitoes, beer,
cigarette smoke.

And those memories folded over themselves into the complicated
Origami of the past
Are overwhelmed by the river as I make the turn to the larger,
        slatted wood bridge.
The same river that I swam in, fished in, hid from work near.
But of course it isn't the same, a river is constantly different but
        always what it wants to be.

There is the tree we jumped from, the broken dam that always
        scared me,

The large, rusted iron wheel above the irrigation ditch,
The river disappearing into the dark as the road lifts up to the left,
That's Meg's house, there, and Bob's behind,
Someone lived down that muddy drive, who was that?
And then the place where the road crosses the stream without a name
And the hill bringing me back to Kapaʻa Stream,
Now the boundary of the farm, and up to the right
The river is darkness, blocking out the hours, days, weeks
I spent up there at the little waterfall, the swimming hole,
the plateau of smooth rock worn down by how many rainstorms,
Sitting, checking traps, swimming, being by myself,
Hearing Pantalon's wife walk from her watery grave
And not quite convincing myself it was just a story.
And up the hill again to the top of the farm bordered by
Pantalon's Road,
Always loud with chicken fights and Sandra lived down there,
        but she's gone now,
Her ex-husband finally in jail,
And that's Sparrow's house, who visited almost daily with his
        cranberry vodka and his potbelly and broken slipper
        shuffle, not much like the namesake bird,
Then that house we built on the land we cleared
And the road continues on before bending back around the now
        dry reservoir
And more folded moments unfurl as I bike past.
My father stuck in the mud,
Kawika finding worms,
Sara mad because I wouldn't share the good pole,
The *Hustler* mag, (was it *Honcho?*) that I found in the abandoned car.
The recent rains filled the reservoir up again, for the first time
        that I recall,
But it isn't really what it was.

I wonder who even remembers what it was.
It's just muddy water over tall grass.

And now my back is to the mountain, to my childhood,
To the river that is the same, always different, raising my
            daughters now
To fish, to swim, to sit, to be alone together.
But when I get home, I'll have to wash my hands for 20 seconds,
And soon I won't have to remind them to wash theirs
Every time we return.
How long will it take for time to cover the scars of 2020?

March 30, 2020

Today I drove a car
For the first time in a while.
We had to go to town, to make two stops.
First to pick up some journals from Kanuikapono
And then to put air in the tires.
A car with no tires is no use but really,
Where are we going to drive on this island
If things get worse?
I suppose the other reason we headed out today
Was simply to put some air in our lungs
And maybe some salt on our faces,
Maybe just to walk
        to sweat
                to have some clothes to wash.
I saw more nēnē than planes in the sky today.
More kama'āina than visitors on the path.
More rusted TOYOs than shiny rentals

On the roads.
And more roadblocks and police checkpoints
Than tour buses.

No tour buses today. Not one.
No cruise ships, either.
Probably also no one selling coconuts at the waterfalls
Or paintings of chickens in the parking lots full of chickens.
But late last night I did see a wild pig, no surprise in my neighborhood,
But this one was digging around in my trashcan.
That seemed new to me, a trashcan pig.

And also today,
A few students sent me emails
To tell me what they've been reading,
To say hello,
To say, "I'm here. I'm awake, safe (maybe)."
To ask me "When will we see each other again?"
To say "I'm annoyed. Worried."
Or to say, "I care, too," which is what I said to them,
Over and over, that last week.

And also today my senator emailed me four times
To share some new piece of news with us,
The lonely masses,
Those left here, finally,
On the rocks in the Pacific,
Which hasn't been peaceful much this year,
Brown yet again, like burnt coffee,
Like Pete's Sumatra, the waves are still rolling in to meet
The sands, the rocks, the river mouths wide open,
The rolling logs and branches washed down from Makaleha,

Waiʻaleʻale,
Kalalea.

From up here on Ea Road, perched above the coast,
The sea fades from dark brown to caramel,
To yellowy and orange then somehow teal and finally,
It becomes blue
Just before the horizon swallows what I see of the sea.

If the view from this year is really perfect,
Which direction are we looking?
Are we looking back, after the scales have fallen,
Are we looking back with unobscured eyes and minds
From some year in the future?
2057, maybe, when the poisons of this world have finally been laid
        to rest?
When the lies and hatred have been put aside?

Do we have 2020 vision right now or will this year be a note
To a time and place I might never see?

April 9, 2020

What is your favorite number?
21, 3 sevens.
3 and 3, could be
6 or thirty-three . . .
. . . or nine.
But I like 27, two 7s.
Odds, but even too.
That's also why I give 14 a pass.

And what is your favorite color?
Green.
Purple.
Blue.
But I like all the colors, sometimes,
Or a color that doesn't have a word for it,
Something like water and light,
Something like the feeling of a favorite number.

And I learned once that color
Is just light that isn't absorbed by an object.
Color is what bounces off of something,
Unused,
But useful to those with eyes.

And I learned once
That numbers don't end.
That they go on forever
And that forever comes in different sizes,
Like the forever that never reaches the end of the universe
And the forever between 2 and 1,
Or between this step and that.

My favorite color is the color of the sea
When I lose track of the various numbers
That measure a day:
Time
        And tide
Order
        And amount
Date

And latitude

My favorite color is when you ignore
The numbers on the "paint by" picture.
My favorite number
        Is four, right now.
The walls, the family,
The seasons, the tides,
The quarters of the moon,
Cardinal directions,
Primaries plus one.

April 13, 2020

Linda "LT" Smith calls them "Hawaiian Lemons,"
Though I doubt their place on the wa'a.
She also once told me about her disdain
For papaya, a tangent from her disdain for the VP.

There is a lemon tree behind my classroom,
Limbs perpetually heavy with the think-skinned fruit
And right now there is a bowl, two actually, in my house
Overfull with dozens of those imperfectly perfect orbs.

When I left on March 13, I thought to pick a few extra, for Erin,
But did not think to bring my potted plants home,
Or to bring anything home, besides an arm full of those lemons.
I'm lucky to be able to visit the tree, both of us in our own
        isolations,
And I bring a backpack this time, not sure of a return trip.
I fill it up, counting to 20, then zipping the backpack closed

And still reaching for five or six more.

When I pick them, I stand under the tree,
Its branches hanging low all around me,
And I reach for the ones that are shades
Of greens and yellows.
The citrus oils stain my skin with a spicy aroma
Belying the sweet tang of their juice,
Perfect for soda water, or tonic,
Or just iced,
Or with whiskey and maple and mint, shaken.

And now we share what we have with people we call neighbors,
Become more neighborly as our isolation stretches on,
And I still wonder about the name of these lemons
As I wonder about a time I can hand one to a friend
Instead of placing it in a bowl on the ground
And stepping back to safety.

It will be nice to make a drink from one
And then pass that drink to a friend
Or neighbor
And to not stand back but to allow our fingers to touch
And to not care about anything but the lemon in the glass
And maybe the sunset.

April 14, 2020

As I sit here, looking out my window,
Listening,
Sitting in the room where I stay,

I understand that we've all started new lives,
Alone together.

Together in aloneness in our own rooms,
And I wonder if my students
Notice the birds are singing more
And if they notice the sound of the waves that I hear
Washing through my open window.

And I think about the cool water
In Kapaʻa Stream
Running over the gray rocks
Making that constant sound
That calms my daughters,
On its way down to the sea, becoming the waves
That I can hear washing
Through my open window.

Listening right now feels like
Hoping we can hear each other soon.

April 17, 2020

There is no traffic until I'm halfway there.
It starts as I near Halfway Bridge, conveniently.
I see blurs of road and sky and tree,
Gray and blue and green,
And then taillights, and I'm slowing,
And then we all stop, together now in that proverbially long line
      of cars.
Stopped, we have something in common.

Is this a quarantine checkpoint?
An accident?
Road work?
The flow of traffic in the opposite lane
Suggests road work, or tree trimming, alternating lanes
        somewhere ahead,
And then we lurch forward, into the shade
That always cools and hides that section of roadway
Between the top of the hill and the bridge.

I pass a masked man in an orange vest,
Leaning on his SLOW sign,
As if any of us had a choice to move quickly;
Nothing moves quickly right now.
We have time to make eye contact and wave.
And I can't tell if anyone is smiling anymore.

I roll down the hill, deeper into the cool,
Orange cones on my left, protecting the yellow and dusty-red
        machinery,
Protecting the other men in masks, in orange.
At this speed I have time to look deeply into the trees,
To wonder about that muddy path,
To notice the smell of crushed eucalyptus,
To hear the sound of water over rocks, running under the road,
To see the root hanging from the inside tread of the front loader.
At this speed, I have time to look deeply
And notice.

On the left, between the small trailer and the guy with the machete
I see the worker with the shovel stop his shoveling.

He looks around a bit, ahead of him into the brush.
He focuses and is still for a moment.
He is dappled by sunlight.
He turns to his left, a half turn,
And bends over the guard rail
To smell a grimy ginger leaning through the tangle of flora there,
The tangle that creeps and threatens every road on Kaua'i.
He lifts the ginger to his face and breathes deeply,
Shakes his head, breathes out,
Grabs another hanging blossom and smells again,
And then he slowly shovels more dirt.

At this speed, right now, one thing we have is time.

May 3, 2020

I found it on my first day back,
The lemon tree,
Tucked away behind the bathrooms,
Under a row of unruly African tulip,
Strangler fig, and java plum.

I also found an ancient plumeria
And rows and rows of green ti.
The tree was covered in flowers
And knobbly, thick skinned fruit
When I found it late last July.

I picked one,
Convinced it was no good,
And the air immediately filled with the scent

Of lemon oil,
A sharp contrast to the thick
And sickly smell of blossoms,
Rotted leaves, and plum.

Over the year, my harvest increased
As my wife's requests did,
From one at a time to a handful,
Then maybe 6 or 7
And now as many as I can fit
In my backpack.

Last week I carefully drove past
The orange cones,
Down the hill and past the groundsperson
Squatting at the side of the driveway,
Peering at me with suspicion in her eyes
Just visible above her mask.
I looked away and eased the truck past.

The grass is taller each time
I have visited since March 13.
This time it is up to my chest.
My legs itch the whole ride home
And the nicks and cuts from the blades
Sting when I shower.
But the smell of lemon,
When I pick up my bag,
When I scratch my legs,
When I think about my school,
When I look across the bowl at my family,
Makes me smile and hope to visit

The tree again.

June 12, 2020

I am not offended when you sit outside,
Or are quiet or don't know me.

I'm not hungry right now; I ate earlier
And I was full, but now I'm not.
I hope you have food to eat.
I am not a plant-based diet,
Or an island.

I'm not a rope, or a tie, or anything
That dangles to adorn a person's face,
Like a smile or eyes or so many freckles.

I am not a face.

I'm not a body or a surfer or a teacher
Or a writer.
I am not a carpenter, but I build things sometimes:
Sentences, boards, rooms.
Things to sit on or to stand in or to read.
I'm not interested in the book you are reading.
I have one here about libraries, which I am not.

I'm not a body but I use my body
To surf, to swim.
I am not the ocean but I am mostly water,
My heart and brain are 73% water.

My lungs 83%.
Even the air is mostly water, all around us, in our lungs, our gills.
But I am not a fish, how could I be?

I am not aware of where the tide is right now,
Six hours behind the moon, always tugging
On the oceans inside of us.
I am not the eel in the tide pool
And I am not my daughters' delighted screams,
But I am delighted.

I am not you.
I am not my students.
I am not a tree or the places where people lived or died.
I am not Breonna, George, Trayvon, Medgar, Fannie, Emmitt,
Tamir, etc., infinity.
And I am not surprised, anymore.
They were all mostly water, too, like me
And like you.
We are not each other but we can know each other, can't we?
Hold each other, can't we?

I am not the rotting food in the sink
And I am not my wife's frustration when she sees it.
I am not a machine, either, or a bird, or timelessness,
Or anything with feathers.
I can think of all the things I am not
And I can know that most of us are mostly water
And we need water
Like we need each other.

June 21, 2020

The sand at the beach
Depends on the beach
It is leftovers, the end of the circle of matter,
Just crushed shells,
Houses of beings who have long ago moved on
It is recycled, ground coral,
Broken pieces of spines or bone or tooth
Piled up on the sea floors, on the edges of land, not quite land itself
It is fine, or coarse, like yellow or white silt or multicolored pebbles
Some sand shows you what it was
Allows you to peer into the ages
And places it came from, the edge of that reef
Or an island long eroded under the waves
Some sand shakes off when you stomp
Your foot at the car door
And some stays with you for hours,
Days,
Appearing when you clean an ear,
Or run your hand through your hair,
Wipe your palm across your eyes,
Or when you sweep the floor of a room that is far from the shore
How much sand have I swallowed,
Tumbling in the sea? Sitting on a towel,
Eating a picnic of chips, dip, peanut butter and veggies,
        and sand, of course
How much has disappeared into my clothes,
Towels, the floors of cars?
The sand at the beach
Depends on the beach
I was raised on an island of them,

On a planet of beaches fringing the specks of land that rudely
Interrupt the sea
I was raised by the shore,
The shore raised us, tempted us into jumping from tree limbs
And dunes,
Warmed our backs as we found respite from the wind, the water,
It caked the corners of our eyes,
Polished our skin
And it says to us "I am moving. Are you?"

SHAREEN K. MURAYAMA

A CONCRETE POEM
SELF-IDENTITY

Asian

aZHen

A-shen

Ayzhen

Eh-ghen

Aay-jen

American

SHAREEN K. MURAYAMA

STICKS, STONES, & WORDS: A TOURIST JUMPED IN WAIKĪKĪ, NOVEMBER 2013

Some words hurt more
the break-up
the in-laws
unemployment rate
than others
the morning-after pill
a suicide
transients
the state with the least recorded
hate crimes
the broken nose
the broken cheekbone
the staples in his head
the begging
the money that fell
from his pocket

I. MESSED. UP.

Right away you could tell somebody had gotten to this guy. His somber white Bro face and Eminem buzz cut filled the YouTube screen with pure fear. His voice quaked. A first-take phone video, but the words had all obviously run through his brain again and again in that awful way your mind races to just *make this all go away*. He'd look away for a second to piece together a sentence, and then talk back into his screen in the tone of somebody who hadn't slept in days: "This was never supposed to be like this. As soon as people started to get really angry, started to see posts about us traveling . . . in Travel Hacks . . . that wasn't like a . . . um . . . message for people to come to Hawai'i . . . I know that's how it was taken . . . "

And look at the title he gave it: I period Messed period Up period.

Wait a minute—was this Baltimore Brett? The same guy from . . . what was the shiny name of his whatever-the-fuck-they-do Bro Company Facebook page?

Hell yeah, Brett! You *did* period Mess period Up period, boy! I don't like to laugh at the misfortune of others, but in a frying-pan-to-the-head cartoon way, the image of a guy like you blubbering away on YouTube is the funniest thing I've scrolled on all day. Nice beard! What, spending a bit of time flat on your back staring at the ceiling, Bro? Feeling too hopeless to even *shave*?

Man, did it feel great just to heckle the guy while he stammered away. I mean, nobody would argue that this idiot didn't have it coming. By now everybody from Hilo to Hanapēpē knew his face from the Facebook and Gram shares, the forwards, the screenshot reposts that only a day and a half earlier had gone . . . well . . . are you still allowed to say it?

Gone viral.

Had it only been three days since some kind of ingrained millennial selfie impulse had pushed Baltimore Brett here into that ill-fated strategy to market . . . *Me!* . . . ? Back then a cloth mask may have covered his face, but there was no mistaking it now from the FB shots: three *winning* faces smiling in Bro-victory, spread socially distant inside one of those airliners now so empty you could see right through it. Scroll down: Bro's on a completely empty sun-drenched Waikīkī beach, he's *crushing it*: "I OWN Hawaii!" How about a whole collage of the beachfront Airbnb he and his "team" scored, *checking in* in Hauʻula, hashtag paradise, hashtag nevergoinghome. Within five minutes no less than eight of my friends had shared the posts, all from a company page called— that's what it was: *Uprooted Platinum.*

The whole thing was so *haole* that normally nobody would have even noticed. Everybody knew that twenty percent of Oʻahu Airbnb owners owned more than twenty houses each and lived . . . elsewhere. The blue-tarp homeless camps ringing the island had long since become part of the scenery, many of them within walking distance of this guy's tropically painted converted hotel-of-a-house where somebody's aunty had grown up a generation ago. The event's whole racial make-up even evoked more of a tired here-we-go-again feeling. ("Typical of his kind" was the worst it got, repeated again and again in the comments.) Precisely two centuries since the whalers and missionaries had #nevergoinghome'd it, even a month earlier a few look-at-me-here-in-paradise selfie brags might have faded into just another dog-bites-man anecdote not worth sharing.

But not this time. Not with the nearest tiny rural hospital waiting to be swamped by maybe hundreds of critically ill patients *who already lived here,* half the state now unemployed in a sincere effort to *flatten the curve*. Not in a place that had seen hundreds of thousands of people die from pandemics, that had once deliberately burned Chinatown to the ground in effort to stop one. Even if you were leaning toward the Tinfoil Hat side of conspiracy-theorizing the whole PlanDemic, well, either you shut down or you didn't, and Hawai'i had. All the kids are home from school, the only place where many of them even get a solid meal, and here comes this *haole*. Picture him: millennial-office-casual-hoodied there in Uprooted Platinum's communal office space up in . . . Baltimore? There he is, interrupting their final face-to-face meeting with the rebellious crack of a microbrew from the well-stocked company fridge, and he comes up with it: Fuck this—if we're gonna work remotely, let's work *remotely*. Like, take a look at these airfares, Bro! Or should I say, *brah*.

The guy was such a cliché that I'd started thinking maybe the whole thing was some kind of hoax. Hawai'i had just been rocked, after all, with three different anti-development movements, each one a clinic in textbook nonviolent demonstration. In response, the hired PR firms had pulled out all the stops trying to trade on a tired stereotype: The Angry Hawaiian. Opposition leaders were constantly being baited and then scrutinized for that one moment when they might lose their patience, just *say* something even a little angry. And here comes the Uprooted team (for the life of me I couldn't figure out exactly what Uprooted even *does*), in the middle of a worldwide pandemic, plastering their Facebook page with . . . well . . . had they actually gone out and done some *research* on what would piss off Hawaiians the most?

The only other explanation was that yes, they were indeed that dumb. Didn't know their dream home was right down the road from Hawaiian Homestead land, one of the few pockets of the whole state left where an indigenous middle-class family could still afford to live, now three and four generations to a three-bedroom spec home. Didn't know Hauʻula from Honolulu. The overthrow? Captain Cook? Wait a minute, Bro, that was *years* ago, I didn't take your land, Bro, let me *explain it to you.*

Still angry at the guy's total ignorance, I'd shared the multiple pics myself, and also joined the long line of irate message senders: "You self-entitled A-holes. Go home. Seriously."

And so he had.

To prove it, Baltimore Brett was now panning his phone camera around a dismally bland gray suburban yard "not in Hawaiʻi," as if maybe Krystal had in fact shared my post with her family in Hauʻula, who'd then shared it with somebody else. More likely the guy had been . . . paid a visit . . . long before his *winning* face had ever shown up on my screen. Listen to him go on about "threats" and "anger" and "I don't know what we were thinking."

I had to laugh again. You could tell from the bags under his eyes that he had in fact been threatened. But had the guy's life actually ever been in danger? The one uncle I did know from up that side was a teddy bear. If Baltimore Brett had been scared off by a taro farmer now in his late sixties, it could only have been because somebody had juiced him up with the same Hawaiians-hate-haoles warning that had once caused a federal agent named Christopher Deedy, brave on his very first night of Waikīkī drinking, to pull his gun and kill a "threatening" kanaka maoli named Kolin Elderts—a racist reaction shared by the (*local*) jury that went on to acquit him of all charges. Thus prompted, a mere scolding from somebody like, say, Uncle Haywood Kalima could have sent him running all the way back to Baltimore.

Like that time Uncle Haywood had to . . . remind . . . a Kailua couple to clean up after their dog at Kaiona Beach Park, a Waimānalo community gem he and his friends had rescued from ruin back in the '90s. Registering him only as some random brown person rather than the same man from last time, a man whose roots in the area extend into the hundreds of years, the couple walked away muttering about their "rights" on a "public beach," armed now with a good victim story about having "gotten attacked," when Uncle had only gotten riled up because letting your dog shit all over a beach in somebody else's community while even as you walked, little kids were digging moats around their sandcastles, well . . . Uncle Haywood had been at least as *baffled* as pissed off.

I'd first met Uncle over twenty years ago, not in Waimānalo, but in the Kokugikan, the Tokyo arena where professional sumo tournaments are held. Even at 52, the thick-muscled man could have stepped into the ring himself and done a little damage. His sons George and Bumbo were two of an astounding *six* young Waimānalo Hawaiians who'd flown all the way to then-famously xenophobic Japan to try a career in their national sport. To make it at all you had possess a samurai sense of restraint called *hinkaku*, believed unavailable to non-Japanese. Outside the ring the Kalima boys were constantly being . . . baited . . . scrutinized . . . for that one moment when they might . . . lose patience . . . just *say* something even a little angry. Uncle Haywood was in Tokyo to watch George's final tournament. It didn't take long for me to figure out that if *hinkaku* had come easily for the Kalima boys, it was because their dad had drilled it into them since small-kid time.

Hinkaku, right to the end. Bumbo explained it all just yesterday when he called to let me know that Uncle Haywood had passed. See, Bumbo's dad had felt chest pains. Fatigue. And he'd decided to not go to Castle Hospital. Instead he went back to his room to try to sleep it off. Massive heart attack at the age of 73. And sure, some of you are shaking your heads, *hahd-head, he neva go docta.* But Uncle Haywood wasn't like that. Back when he was in his late fifties-early sixties, he seemed to be going to funerals every time I ran into him. "Gotta get your ass checked," he would tell me.

"Go docta, check your ass." He himself went regularly. Watched what he ate. His hours at the beach kept him supremely fit for a man decades younger. But this time he didn't go. We were in the middle of a global pandemic. Other people needed the hospital, the attention of the doctors and nurses, the bed and possibly the ventilator he would have been taking up. Somebody could die.

At that very moment, Typical-of-his-kind Baltimore Brett's just-about-*private* jet was touching down at HNL.

Look at him now going on about "We didn't realize this was going to be such a huge thing." He's telling us how "the Internet's a crazy place for it to go from one person to thirty thousand people in an hour." He's drifting away from the point of his title now, talking about "a witch hunt," and the sudden need for "security guards."

Social . . . distancing . . . at its finest. If I didn't know you any better, Brett, I might think you'd been taught that you were *supposed* to lace your apologies with a little situation-explaining and my-siding. You an only child, Brett? All the way from your everybody-gets-a-trophy soccer days and through that prep school and a grade-inflated econ degree ("We're paying a lot of money for this"), on through to the frat-boy-connected company you started? All on your own? Without a . . . trust fund? Is the whole thing always all about—

Wait a second . . .

". . . and nobody at the business was prepared for that," the flood of emails, messages, calls.

And what's this?

". . . and it was only three of us that actually went, and everyone's being affected . . . and I hope that people can forgive us." Brett! Are you actually *empathizing* with other human beings? I know you're talking mainly about your irate coworkers back in

... Baltimore ... but hey, it's a start! Tell me: has the perfect storm of a global pandemic, with massive amounts of misfortune spread far and wide, plus that sense of *fear for your life* that got you on the *next plane home* "at 8:44," plus the absolute worst enemy of an arrogant white man's peaceful happy life—*Public Humiliation!* And on such a scale!—has it all added up to *also* get you to understand what Uncle Haywood Kalima knew his whole life?

That little flicker of empathy—it actually got me thinking there may be hope for the guy after all. I mean, he did kick this whole thing off with That period Unequivocal period Title of his. So was it too much of a stretch to believe that over the course of his many recent sleepless hours, Brett here had finally bothered to Google exactly what the flock had been going on in Hawai'i for the past ten months? Could we hope that maybe somebody'd pm'd him a list of links about the plan to turn Sherwood's in Waimānalo into park service for Kailua's swarm of Airbnb tourists? About the dozens of windmills suddenly towering over Kahuku elementary schools? About the TMT?

The Thirty Meter Telescope: the Indigenous Serving Institution-branded University of Hawai'i fronts an outside investor aiming to erect the island's tallest building right in the middle of one of the state's most culturally sensitive areas so that important discoveries can be made by astronomers from ... the University of California. That one, too, had had all the ingredients: in lock-step with the pro-development state government, TMT Corporation spends over a decade dumping *millions of dollars* worth of PR all over the state: It's for scientific discovery! It's for the keiki! Allow me to wedge you into the position of having to choose between your kid's future and your centuries-old cultural beliefs: here's a THINK scholarship!

Sure enough, after two exhausting contested case hearings hammering home the state law prohibiting construction that is "adverse and significant" in any conservation district, the eighteen-story UCAL project is green-lighted by the state's hand-picked hearings officer. By a 4-1 vote, the Supreme Court rejects the appeal, with the dissenting justice *laying waste* to TMT's argument that its twenty-acre footprint can't be considered "significant" because more than a dozen telescopes *already* pollute Mauna Kea's summit.

Had Baltimore Brett since read up on the TMT? Had he seen one of the many YouTube videos professionally produced by volunteers for the *kiaʻi*, the mountain's protectors, detailing last July's demonstration to ensure that the State of Hawaiʻi follow *its own laws*? Again: all the usual ingredients. All the way back through the SuperFerry to the H-3 freeway to one hotel or military base after another built right on the very bones of kānaka maoli. Hawaiians had stood in front of every one of those sell-outs to outsiders, too. Some had gotten killed for it.

Except this time it was different. Way different.

I could see that myself one morning a couple of weeks into the action when I drove up the Mauna to lend a little support with a couple of shopping bags of Safeway sandwiches. Pretty much every face among the many hundreds up there was Hawaiian. (No, not *local*. Hawaiian. Kānaka maoli.) They'd converted the vast parking area at the base of the kīpuka into a city of crowded wedding-grad-party-sized tents. Clear signage pointed out where to go for the day's newly instituted Puʻuhuluhulu University classes. The Mauna Medics tent—a M.A.S.H. hospital, really, where you had to produce credentials and pass a strict orientation just to volunteer. KAPU ALOHA signs everywhere listed the strictly enforced rules of nonviolent demonstrations essential to the effort's success. Another sign listed supplies needed for donation, and those no longer needed. A working kitchen rivaling that of any restaurant buzzed with activity. A system for handling waste was set up near the Porta Potties the whole place as free of trash as Uncle Haywood Kalima's Kiona Beach Park.

I went up to the Orientation tent to give them my sandwiches, and here's what they said: "You hungry? They serving breakfast inside that tent right over there."

Across the highway (a team of fluorescent-suited professional traffic controllers armed with those SLOW/STOP signs tightly monitored the crossing), well . . . if the kīpuka side looked like a well-organized baby lūʻau, the Mauna side was a family reunion, all anchored by the gray roofline of the Kupuna Tent now spanning the Access Road. They'd set it up just downslope from the cattle guard the demonstrators had chained themselves to on the action's first day—an area now smothered by a herd of heavily armed DLNR cops. Familiar faces dotted the crowd milling around the tent: a colleague from UH who'd turned out to be married to a cousin of my good brother Kaʻimi, who'd built my Dad's house. A former student from Waimea. Kealoha. Leilani. Uncle Jimmy, who'd taught me to paddle canoe.

Coach Fats?

Sure enough. A prison guard who ran the athletic association over on the Keaukaha Homestead, I'd never have picked Coach Fats for an activist. Not like he was one of those guys fed up enough to just dismiss any sort of civic involvement as *politics* . . . or somebody programmed to look down on fellow kānaka maoli unwilling to fully embrace *progress* . . . or one who'd bought into the TMT bribe scheme dumping money on just about every Hawaiʻi DOE school with an elevated kānaka maoli student population. Still, Coach Fats had seemed about as far removed as possible from an upside-down flag, and yet here he was: holding space up on the Mauna.

"And I'd like you to meet my wife Janet," he said. "This is Kenny's dad."

Kenny is my son Kensuke. Back when his coach-pitch team dissolved and left him without a place to play, every day for a week I drove to all six Hilo fields to find him a new home. Nobody even pretended to want him. It was just, "Sorry, we're full."

Finally I drove to the Homestead in Keaukaha.

"We don't have any spots either," I was told. And then this: "But he's more than welcome to practice with us. He just won't be playing in any of the games."

A couple of days later we were back. Within seconds Kensuke was christened with his Homestead name: "Kenny!" And not once did a single kid ever tell him he sucked, or that he wasn't really on the team. Over the summer enough Homestead kids joined so they were able to split Kenny's age group into two teams, and that's where I first met Coach Fats, who clearly presided over all four diamonds. He stood 5'9" in both height and width—he's since samurai-dieted down over a hundred pounds, and I call him "Coach Slim." But the real imposing part about Fats was his mouth: "JOSHUA! RUN THE WHOLE PAHK! NOW!" "MAKA! YOU NOT SELLING LAND OUT THERE!" Each season began with an elaborate opening ceremony and ended with a potluck. Coach Fats would always conclude with solemn request for all of the players to thank their parents, and to remember that when kids and parents alike put on their jerseys or even their hats, everybody was looking at them (scrutinizing?)—they're representing the whole Keaukaha Homestead family.

We would only truly learn what Coach Fats meant by all this a couple of years later, when the bruises started appearing all over Kenny's legs, arms, chest, face. I'd just thought it a sign of an active childhood. But my wife Noriko, an ICU nurse, insisted on a blood test. The results were waiting in my inbox at 5:00 one morning, a page-long list of red numbers and arrows pointing down, WBC, RBC, Platelets . . . is that Red Blood Cell? Google said he might have leukemia. A bone-marrow biopsy on Oʻahu said it was something called aplastic anemia. There's no treatment. It would either get better on its own with "spontaneous improvement," or it would drop further and he would either get a bone marrow transplant, or die. In the meantime, a severe cut or compound fracture, and he could bleed out, especially way out here in rural Hilo. A concussive blow to the head could give him a stroke. At ten years old.

The only time I ever saw Kenny cry over this horrifying news was not at Kapiʻolani Hospital, its Pediatric Ambulatory Unit crowded with kids his age bald from chemo treatment. It was the day we drove to practice and I told him I had to let his coaches know.

I found Coach Shaka Kev and asked if he had a minute, and that was, I think, the only time I cried: when his face morphed into this look of total concern, as if we were talking about *his* kid, the moment I said the word "medical." Within the hour Tank's mother Krystal was organizing a bone marrow drive. A meeting was set up: Kenny, us, and all the coaches and team moms from tee-ball on up. The whole room sobbed when Noriko explained it, linebacker-sized braddas blubbering away, Coach Bronson standing up and saying "Let's go, Kenny! I give you my bone marrow right now!" With any other team on the planet, the meeting's purpose would have been to see if it was feasible to keep the player involved and to outline the potential liabilities and their impact on the organization both now and in the future since we could be setting precedent here that will affect us moving forward—either that, or to make a show of concern while you figured out a way to blame the doctors when you cut him. But Coach Fats had made up his mind long before knowing any of the details about aplastic anemia. He'd called the meeting because he wanted everybody to help Kenny get better. "We'll do whatever you folks are comfortable with," he said. "Kenny, you're part of our team. We're family here."

By season's end, Kenny's platelet count had doubled. You should have seen him dance around last Thursday—another year later—when it had doubled again, right up close to normal range.

Up on the Mauna, I was so thrilled to meet Coach Fats's wife, if only so I could finally share with Aunty Janet our gratitude for her son Coach Ihi, Kenny's coach for the rest of that year. Ihi had been the one to ease off on the bullets he routinely shot at his players' legs for ground ball practice when it was Kenny's turn, to hold his tongue when Kenny failed to slide during base running drills, to explain to the opposing coach why the right fielder was wearing a helmet, to remind the umpire to start the inning with one out when Kenny, who wasn't allowed to face a seventh grader firing from less than fifty feet away, was set to lead off.

About six months into the season Kenny jogged past my spot next to the right field grass, stopped, looked right at me. His boyz had just finished demolishing a short lefty lobbing it in so slow the kid couldn't have done much damage had he nailed anyone right in the face. He couldn't take it anymore. For the very first time my stoic son finally said it: "Dad! Can I *hit*? Please!"

By then only two distinct thoughts ever shot around my brain: *What are the chances?* And, *He could die!* We'd flown all the way to Philadelphia, home of the top pediatric bone marrow failure center in the world. I'd burned hour after hour online studying diet and supplement impacts on platelet counts, spent oh-so-much energy trying to just *make this all go away*. I mean, he wasn't even supposed to be out there.

I gave him a nod anyway. "Yeah boy. Swing that bat."

When the inning ended, the dugout erupted at his news, ten kids all trying to out-scream each other: "Kenny, use my bat!" "Kenny, use *my* bat!" He stepped into the box for the first time in months looking so *locked in* that you could tell what was going to happen next: a total feast on the first pitch he saw, lined hard into left field. Again the dugout erupted, right here in the third inning, like they'd won it all. Kenny eventually wound up on third, and they would have won the game, too, except that Coach Ihi held him up on a ball that got past the catcher, worried about what a collision at the plate might do to him.

"There have been reports of drug use on the Mauna."

You can find that one on YouTube, too, but it's not Baltimore Brett. Listen to how effortlessly those words roll off the tongue of . . . Governor David Ige. Way back around the time Uncle Haywood was spearing an eighty-pound ulua off Kiona with his three-prong (my favorite Mr. Kalima legend), and Coach Fats was teaching his young boy Ihi how to hit off a tee, David Ige was setting off from Pearl City to build a steady career as a no-make-waves State Capitol Lifer. To see him up at the podium now in abject fear ("They're all making fun of my voice!") evoked the image of that guy at the very last desk in the back corner of the Planning Department—the one too scared to go help anybody at the counter—getting tapped on the head by his Fairy Godmother to become governor of the whole state.

"My first concern is the safety of the people, and to prevent violence." Fozzie said that, too. (As if to sharpen the insult, most of his constituents called him "Kermit" when his voice actually matched that of a different Muppet altogether, Fozzie Bear.)

"There are waste facilities that are insufficient for the amount of people." Yes, he said that, too.

"People are running back and forth across a busy highway." Said that.

And finally, "There are different groups, and no one is in charge."

Governor Ige read all of this from a *prepared statement*. And he hit every single bullet point on The Pearl City Grandma List: Hawaiians are lazy violent druggies who are always fighting with one another and trashing the environment. He was so efficient that at first I'd thought it was a PR ploy designed to try to dirty up the opposition.

But then it reminded me of something else: a scene I once made up where a state senator named Russell Lee imagines the thoughts of another character I made up, the local (not Hawaiian, not kānaka maoli) Marisa Horiguchi. At a fundraiser for a local drug treatment center, the two of them are watching hula performed by a tattered collection of recovering addicts, every one of them Hawaiian, when Russ catches sight of this young woman's look of *approval* from across a hotel ballroom.

"She *approved* because she'd been raised to never have any expectations for Hawaiians in the first place . . . programmed to *look down* since all the way back in high school, if not before, when her mother had given her a list of acceptable *ethnicities* for boyfriends, in order: local-Japanese, Japanese, local-Chinese (4th generation or higher), and if it turned out to be otherwise unavoidable, haole. Absent from the list were Filipinos, Micronesians, and most especially, Hawaiians. Hawaiians were lazy, violent, inarticulate, and ignorant."

The thing is, Russ wasn't making this up. *I* wasn't making this up. I'd copied it verbatim out my memory of having heard it recited to me on more than one very uncomfortable occasion, always by somebody who had "lived here for generations." Somebody *local*.

Local.

And by 2019, it was Governor David Ige—not Uncle Haywood, not Coach Fats—who had come to epitomize *local*, the us-guys cultural marker born of the Pidgin that had once united Hawai'i's famous ethnic mix of sugar plantation workers into the collective force strong enough to take down their Big Five haole oppressors. He'd gone from being waited upon in Pearl City Sunday Dinner comfort (simultaneously being taught to trade on the heroic past of cutting sugarcane all day in the hot sun), to dutifully passing through UH along the way to the state legislature and now the capitol's fifth floor, the very poster boy for what had long since become Hawai'i's political ruling class. Never mind that David had likely never set foot on an actual sugar plantation, or that if he ever did speak Pidgin, it was of the Guy Hagi Wedding Toast variety. He was local!

Haunani had warned about it decades ago, what *local* had actually come to mean.

Sure enough, by the time the governor stood at the podium to deliver Grandma's List from his *prepared statement*, David Ige— even more than those lazy drug-addicted thugs up on the Mauna— guys like *David Ige* had become the ones with the *birthright to Hawai'i*. You want to erect a two-billion-dollar twenty-story industrial development in the middle of a conservation district so a handful of UCAL astronomy assistant professors can get tenure? Well, all you have to do is talk to Governor Ige here. He *owns* Hawai'i! Plantation stock! Born and raised!

Hawaiians?

Trotted out once in a while as our "host culture" for the ho'olaule'a down at your local DOE elementary school so the (*local*) teachers can call themselves *Hawaiian at heart*.

But otherwise erased.

Invisible.

In fact, Governor Ige himself had just proved that it's possible live an entire full life in Hawai'i, *for generations*, without ever having had a meaningful conversation with kānaka maoli. Outside of, say, meetings at the capitol . . . hmm . . . wasn't the teller at the bank the other day named Maile or Malia or something? No, never did play golf with a Hawaiian, or go fishing. Never did bother to read *From A Native Daughter*. Never did go out for beers with anybody Hawaiian. Never been to a baby lū'au, grad party, wedding, funeral on the Homestead. Hard to find any Hawaiians really . . . qualified . . . for a position on my staff.

Which is why when Grandma's List flowed from his mouth in such efficient fashion (even with that *voice*), it wasn't some kind of rhetorical flourish. He wasn't trying to politically undermine what was turning out to be a spectacularly popular movement.

It was a *reflex*.

Just like when his (*local*) coronavirus "incident commander" more recently predicted rioting as a likely response to our shutdown. Like when the Punahou son of a "prominent" (*local*) real estate investor fears personally distributing his cache of donated masks on the Wai'anae coast . . . it's right there in the *Civil Beat* . . . wink-and-a-nod . . . his concerns about *trust issues* . . . ho, gotta love it when one of these guys calls you *haole*.

A *reflex*.

And as it turned out, one that amounted to a huge tactical error.

Thusly blinded, it never once registered to Pearl City Dave that what he really faced up there on the Mauna was some serious brainpower. Among the kumu hula leading morning protocol, and the folks steeped in the kind of Homestead country wisdom spun by Coach Fats and Uncle Jimmy, stood a higher concentration of advanced degree holders than anywhere else in the state. Medical degrees, law degrees, Hawaiian Studies, political science, history and English, philosophy and psychology. Here's Governor Ige promising TMT he'll have no trouble dispersing an angry mob of lazy drug-addicted thugs, when his actual opponents are the most productive scholars the University of Hawai'i has ever produced— not astronomers, but academics from every field even peripherally related to the colonization of indigenous (not *local*) people, or, in this case, *themselves*. Thousands of them. Four generations' worth. Each one full of their share of enough-is-enough anger, yeah, but lockstep in their complete understanding that for any chance of winning the long game, however much you really wanted to score right now, you had no choice but to hold Kenny up at third base.

Look at Governor Ige finally roll up the Mauna in a fleet of SUVs, ensconced inside a full and armed security detail, only to be greeted with *honi* bestowed by a kupuna well north of seventy years old. Look at him drop what eventually added up to *tens of millions* of dollars worth of law enforcement money to ensure that a group of people whose ultimate success depended on nonviolence did not become . . . violent.

Tens of millions of dollars.

And now all of a sudden—man, life can come at you fast, *Baltimore Brett* fast. Just like somebody'd flipped a switch, tax revenue projections drop by the *hundreds of millions of dollars.* Queen Lili'uokalani once had to close Honolulu harbor to *all boat traffic for months* to keep smallpox from decimating her people, but here's Governor Ige so worried about his budget shortfall that he can barely bring himself to address *cruise ship arrivals*, even days after I'd unknowingly paddled my canoe within fifty yards of the *Grand Princess*, the famous ground-zero COVID cruise ship parked right there in Hilo Bay. Airline arrivals? Lacking the political wherewithal to persuade United and Hawaiian to at least do something about their dirt-cheap fares, the best he could do was to "encourage" visitors to postpone their vacations "to a later date," and then finally institute a 14-day quarantine . . . on the *honor system.* Thousands of businesses are shut down, unemployment at fifty percent, mountains of new claims verge on bankrupting the state, and here's Pearl City David scrambling for table scraps, wishing he had some way to get back all that money he'd scattered into the Mauna Kea breeze for months and months and months.

I came home the other day to find my wife staring at her phone and crying, and it wasn't about Uncle Haywood. Or, well, not *directly* about him. As I said, Noriko is an ICU nurse, certified for Critical Care. For the past fifteen years she's been at Hilo Medical Center caring for East Hawai'i's sick and injured, her overall patient load skewed heavily toward folks suffering from heart failure, diabetes, and lung issues—that is, the trifecta of historical trauma-induced health ailments disproportionally affecting kānaka maoli for decades. As we were just beginning to learn, this was the exact same trifecta leading to almost certain death in a patient who has contracted COVID-19, a disease that otherwise comes with an overall survival rate of close to 99%.

"What."

She looked up from the phone: "He wants to cut our pay." By *our* pay, she wasn't talking about herself and me. *Our* meant all of the frontline workers about to risk their lives and those of their families—Noriko's mother-in-law, maybe, an 81-year-old with a severely compromised immune system. Remember Kenny's aplastic anemia? Severely compromised immune system. He's 12.

The longer she sat in silence, the more you knew her total shock had nothing to do with the size of her paycheck. The word "care" is actually part of her professional credential—I've seen her save somebody with chest pains right there on the beach at Richardson's. She knew we were both lucky to still have jobs.

At the same time, here she was in a state where a Sig Zane-clad university president is paid nearly $400,000 annually, only to shill for a (California) corporation and make *himself* the victim when 75-year-old Walter Ritte is chained to a cattle guard for seven hours. ("The most difficult day of my presidency.") Here was Noriko, devoting her life to an island where (yet another California) UH-Hilo chancellor is paid nearly as much to try to rebrand the way an Indigenous Serving Institution might credibly front a corporation willing to put Uncle Jimmy in zip ties. Here was Noriko in a state where an imported university football coach is paid nearly a million dollars when football cannot even be played, and Governor David Ige's *very first solution* to his sudden budget problem is to destroy the morale of the very state employees who had heroically tried to bring Uncle Haywood back to life when he finally did make it to the hospital for a *triple bypass*. During a global pandemic, the governor's very first solution to make up for all the money he'd blown trying to bait a band of peaceful and concerned senior citizens into doing something worthy of a violent state response is to *substantially increase the chances of death* for anybody over the age of . . . sixty . . . with . . . diabetes . . . heart disease.

You have to wonder: was that a reflex too?

Because all the while, the gate down at the airport remains wide open.

Even Baltimore Brett—he never broke any laws. The poster boy of haole entitlement? Sure. Not really thinking? Admittedly. Does his apology veer into the kind of passive language ("our photos were taken the wrong way") normally designed to shift blame and avoid responsibility? From time to time, yes.

But as much as I wanted to nitpick, in the end I had to hand it to Brett. I'd even go so far as to guess that he might have had the decency to post his I-period-Messed-period-Up-period monologue even if he hadn't felt like his life was in danger. (I still don't think it ever actually was, despite what some folks might have expressed in their angry disbelief.)

Look at him conclude, just about holding back tears, not of fear, but of true sincerity, in a dignified way, *humble*, even, with a touch of . . . *hinkaku* . . . clearly for the first time in his life: "Please take that apology and understand that . . . we didn't know what we were thinking. And we never should have been there. I'm so sorry."

Listen to him say his name, right out loud, not Baltimore Brett, but Patrick DeMarsico.

Patrick DeMarsico.

"I'm so sorry."

I mean, for guy like that . . . it's not like Patrick was *local*, after all. Wasn't . . . from here. Wasn't . . . born and raised. 🦎

WEEK 3

As of March 14, 2020, there are a total of 4 confirmed positive test
results for COVID-19 in Hawai'i. Two positive results were announced
today for two visitors on Kaua'i who traveled from Indiana.

—State of Hawaii Department of Health

Over eggs and after a quick study of the recent numbers
my husband teases that only women, *Clearly the stronger sex*
should take care of COVID cases. It's not often we get to
breakfast together, he's been picking up more shifts, short staffed
even with all vacations cancelled. We need to laugh.
He does nights and I'm on days collectively
we puzzle the pieces of confusion that is our work in the hospital now.
We watch the crisis in NY on TV, YouTube solutions from other states
like sewing masks to slow down the hemorrhage of their N95 supply.
Our hospital isn't there yet. On Tuesday a memo was sent out—
we are down to an eight-day ration. The MICU manager is locking
their supply in her office, the angio techs snark about washing them.
Coincidentally, during today's press conference
the president straight-faced suggests this: washing masks.
He's kidding right? I hear my voice echo back from the depths
of my favorite coffee mug when I ask this, I taste its disbelief
as I swallow the last of it. Evasive answers follow from the podium
about arrival dates for needed PPEs and ventilators. This will mean
more email from administration *We are urging our staff to not panic.*
My husband calmly munches the last of his toast no butter
We reminisce about those two patients, in mid-January
their ungodly pneumonias which didn't make sense

100% oxygen for days and then their slow recovery *Do you think?*
Maybe. We hypothesize about our lingering cough last month
over the last strip of bacon. On TV more images of NY
ER doctors in fumigation respirators, a line of people extending
out and around the block in surgical masks and puffy jackets
like a horrible theme park attraction—the sky there deceptively blue.
He heads to bed as I push down the papaya rind into the trash;
his light snore from the bedroom, breadcrumbs on the kitchen floor
the TV droning on astonishingly unextraordinary, comfortable.

ELMER OMAR PIZO

MILKFISH
Honolulu Chinatown

Dollar-forty a pound.
The fish is 3 pounds no more, no less.
Four dollars and twenty cents—
this what cost me
for a frozen milkfish
raised with artificial feed
in an earthen pond
somewhere in the rugged
coast of Taiwan.

Cleaned, descaled,
deboned, butterflied,
I soaked it for a day
in a mixture of vinegar,
soy sauce, and lots
of crushed garlic,
with a minimal sprinkle
of ground black pepper.

When I lifted the fish from
the container to fry it,
what a shocking surprise!

A maggot lost its grip
from the belly's side
and fell back into the marinade!

ELMER OMAR PIZO

KIDNEY STONES

St. Francis Hospital-Waipahu, July 1998

On a scale of 1 to 10, how do you rate the pain?
The emergency physician asked.
It's more than 12, doctor! I replied groaning.

What I said was not an exaggeration.

For stones, big or small;
stones, gray or yellowish green;
stones the size of a corn seed
or half the size of my thumb;
I didn't have any idea on what they really were,
not until I couldn't get myself to pee
on that early morning.

Lying on a gurney without any clothes on
except my underwear, the attendant had only
a white linen cloth draped on my disintegrating body!

To shield me from the biting cold
(the x-ray room's air-con in full blast),
I pulled a part of the cloth up to cover my face.
My left wrist exposed with my medical tag on it.

Keeping still, I waited for my turn to be wheeled
into the MRI tube. On the side of the main door
leading to the x-ray room, two housekeepers

pushed their mops on the floor's surface.
Ayna, kaasi met. Amangan ta natayen!
Commented one of them.
Segurado ka? The other asked.

Ignoring her question, the former prodded
the latter for them to come near me.
She wanted to find out if I was already dead.
Before they could get near to me, I got up
and said: *Agang-angesak pay, Nana!*

Plak! Plak! They dropped their mops to the floor
and charged to the nursing station as fast as they could.
All the while they're screaming: *Nurse, nurse!*
Your patient in the x-ray room! He got up
and told us he just came back from the dead!

Ayna, kaasi met. Oh, my! Sorry for him.
Amangan ta natayen! Maybe he's dead!
Segurado ka? Are you sure?
Agan-angesak pay Nana! I'm still breathing auntie!

ELMER OMAR PIZO

GLOWING IN THE DARK

In 1992, the Environmental Protection Agency placed the Naval Base
Shipyard on a "National Priority List of Hazardous Waste Sites." By 1998,
the Hawai'i Department of Health advised people not to eat fish or shellfish
from the water of Pearl Harbor.

Bait was tiny balls
of spare sweet Hawaiian bread
I threw in the freezer
the other night.

Yesterday,
past 8:00 in the morning,
the white, two-gallon Home Depot bucket
was almost full of tilapia
struggling to catch their breath.

Yesterday evening,
I tossed several of them
in the smoking oil for dinner,
the rest given icy treatment
in the refrigerator's freezer compartment.

Makisig—the cat I rescued behind the Dumpster
at the Long's Drug Store near the 'Ewa Post Office—
and I had them for dinner,
our dipping sauce:
calamansi and bagoong.

Tonight, friends at ʻEwa Beach Park
noticed *Makisig* and I
were like LED lights,
glowing in the dark.

ELMER OMAR PIZO

IMMIGRATION

Roentgen Rays
DoH-TB Control Branch
Lanakila Health Clinic/Leahi Hospital

In 2005, 81.3 percent of the state's new TB cases were non-U.S. born individuals. Persons born in the Philippines accounted for 63.7 percent of the non-U.S. born cases, followed by Japan (6.6 percent), Vietnam (5.5 percent), and the Republic of the Marshall Islands (5.5 percent).

Health Trends in Hawai'i
Hawai'i Health Information Corporation

1. For Chest X-Rated Rays:

If you're a recent immigrant,
please proceed to the reception area
and fill-out an X-rated form.

Once the form is processed,
go to Area 4. That's the X-Rated
Department. You can't miss it.
It's directly across the Coffee-Break
Department.

Once you're in there, grab a number
and have a seat. Wait until your number
is called. As soon as your number
is called, get inside the cubicle
and begin peeling yourself of any
gold attachments.

If you have earrings dangling on your nipples,
take them off. *(Sore? Then leave them just like that.*
Anyway, Drs. Nguyen, Pun, Gollop have the final say about it.)

Because you know what?
Authentic or fake, when those necklaces
and dangling earrings are not removed,
they deflect and overpower the X-rated rays.

2. For a Female Patient:
You need to take off your dress or blouse
Or whatever upper garment you're wearing.
When you're done doing that, put on one
of those blue gowns hanging on the rack.

Remember this now: When you wear it,
the opening must be at the back.
If not, your breasts will be exposed
not only to the rays but to the technician
and his assistant themselves.

Finally, if you're wearing a skirt,
leave it on.

If you're not comfortable removing your dress
or blouse, say it so. Just take this into mind:
For the machine to work best, it's mandatory
for patients to remove their upper garments.

Otherwise, you're required to get those lungs
out of your chest and hand them over the technician.

If you decide to go that way, make it sure
your hands are washed well and disinfected.

But to be honest with you, it's not as simple as
that. You have to be in isolation for a month
like pets coming from other places in the Hawai'i
Department of Agriculture's Animal Quarantine Station.

You'll undergo a lot of tests: your heart, BP,
blood, and state of mind.

A cup of coffee is forbidden.
Going to the restroom is a chore.
All the contraptions on your body
must be taken off before you can stand up.

Before you go through all that,
you have to sign a waiver
releasing all those involved
(doctors, nurses, x-ray guys)
from any responsibility in case
things go awry.

Here's one thing that is so important:
If you're a day or a month pregnant,
or suspect that you are, don't be shy.
Advise any of the attending technicians
about your condition. That way,
they can assist you better, employ
the necessary precautions.

3. For a Male Patient:

The technicians want you to get naked
above the waist. Better leave your pants on.

4. For Both:
If you have a long hair, tie them into a knot
and raise them above your neck.
If you don't, the picture isn't accurate.
You have to do it again.
And this makes you sorry for the rest
of your life. Why? Because it's too risky
to be exposed to X-rated rays a number
of times in just one setting.

When you have gone through all that,
kindly check your ears for wax build-up.
This saves Mr. Bill, Orlando, and Richard
The trouble of being blamed what they
are saying is not clear enough.

5.
During the actual x-ray process,
take a deep breath. If you don't
the X-rated guys are forced to count
your ribs. It's not a nice procedure.
They poke, press, probe through your
tissues. If less than eight on your left
or right rib cages, it means only one
thing: You cheated!

It's imperative you hold your breath
for a few seconds. If you don't, severe
distortions on the picture make it appear

as if your lungs are infected.

Another thing. If you happen to pass gas
while you're holding your breath,
the least you can do is smile and apologize.

How many times I have seen patients
staring at the ceiling, pretending
they were innocent of the crime they
just did. And here we were suffocating
because we couldn't leave and we
had to hold our breath.

Anyway, Mr. Bill is an understanding person.
His Wizard air freshener at the counter
is always on the standby, alert and ready
for this kind of emergency.

That one, he says in the manner
of a seasoned salesman, is dual action.

A single burst destroys, instead
of masking whatever odor is present
in the air, leaving at the same time
a refreshing scent of vanilla,
raspberries and strawberries.

6.
Beeeeppppp!
This whistle-like sound indicates
the picture-taking session is over.
Now, you can step back from the X-rated board

and proceed to the dressing room.

Kindly double-check everything.
It's not a pleasure talking to cops
about missing purses, wallets,
earrings, necklaces, even wigs,
and sorting through tons of rubbish
in the bins to make sure they're not
hidden there.

Once you're done putting all your garments
and jewelries, go back to the waiting area
and have a seat again.
If the waiting area is filled
and doesn't have available seat, don't go out.
Remain standing.
Your name will be called anytime.

Just be patient. Inside the dark room,
Mr. Bill's already holding the film against the light,
checking it for the presence of termite-like holes
disfiguring your lungs.

If Mr. Bill says you can go, that you just wait
for the official result in the mail three to four working days,
then there's nothing to worry about.
No need to ask some more questions.
Just go!

Otherwise, he may change his mind
and tell you to follow him to the doctor.
If it's Dr. Nguyen or Dr. Gollop, you'll be

alright. If Dr. Pon, I'm so sorry.

Upon taking a quick glance at your film,
he tosses your X-rated film to the side.
He stands up, shake your hands as he tells you
with a silly smile: *Congratulations!*
All I see, your ribs but no more lungs!

MAUNAWILI

My brother's room was off the washhouse. Too wild to live inside, he was out there with the centipedes and gardenias. Only in his early teens, he was already a big wave surfer with a sponsorship from a Swiss company called Mistral. They gave him surfboards, and at their house on Lanikai Beach, the Swiss girls sunbathed topless.

I tried to read a book called *Death in Venice* by Thomas Mann. When no one noticed, I gave it up. I couldn't surf for shit.

The Outsiders was playing at the Kailua Drive-In that night. We could have watched it from the roof, heard it on the tin speakers attached to the cars, over the eucalyptus trees. The trade winds were good.

He said come see him.

We lit up a joint and smoked it with a plastic bag over our heads. The Steve Miller Band was playing from a cassette player. "Rock'n Me." The Japanese Zero off the Pali Lookout was still bleeding rust into the clay. Voyager 2 was past Saturn. Reagan was POTUS.

The weed was local with purple and orange hairs on the buds that stuck to your fingers. The resins smelled something lurid.

Then his friends came.

I got in the back with someone else's younger brother. I recognized the look in his eyes. That younger brother look.

Another joint. Another bottle. What the fuck did we know?

We had to pick up some friends down near the city dump, in a subdivision called Enchanted Lakes. The most lifeless of places are named like that.

We were in the second car of doped-up, adrenaline-addicted surfers turning onto the freeway, when the one in front rolled over and slid through the hedge of Castle Hospital. It came to a halt with its wheels spinning toward the clouds.

Kailua boys out of every window like Starsky & Hutch. Then they doubled back on us. My brother looked me in the eyes and said, "You gotta get out." The other younger brother and I were pushed out into traffic. Horns blaring. I crossed the highway, ran up the road, turned left, sprinted through someone's yard, and slid down a hill. I heard sirens approaching in the high grass of Maunawili Valley. 🌀

HŌKŪLANI RIVERA

E HINA

'O kou mo'opuna kēia keiki. Ke kāhea nei 'o ia.
E 'olu'olu, e ho'olohe mai. E 'olu'olu, eō mai.

When she balances along branches of koa canopies, and searches,
beyond that valley
      beyond that city
           beyond that glittering sea—
when she strains across the horizon for
the pu'u/wai of her nation

                      Mauna a Wākea—
she can't help but fill imagination with you. However intangible,
imperceptible—magic.

> *E ku'u kupunahine, did your lauoho flow deep*
> *brown like the waters of the wet season, cracked by lava in just*
> *the right lighting? Did the filaments of your eyes*
> *snare the sun? Or was that*
>
>   *your 'anā'anā,*
> *stirring every shadow, every pō—just like in the*
> *beginning? Did you find your future in your mother's embrace?*
> *And your birth in your daughter's?*

Eō ka 'anā'anā i ke keiki. Kanu 'ia ka mana i kēia pua.
E nāueue ana ka hōnua me ka wahine.

Your silhouette sways through the mist caught
in adolescent koa leaves—she grasps

at the fog, finds a pueo feather in your place.

It's been six years now
She carries it with her, still, anything
to tether—herself
to you
to nuʻu
to mauna

—vibrating
with each pound in a sea of
pahu drums, and steadfast soles,
and kāhea, and heartbeats, and hae/Hawaiʻi

And she wonders if
you're watching.

*E kuʻu kupunahine, are your eyes the stars themselves? Should I
be looking for you there?
Are your hands the sweet winter winds, coaxing us back
to our homelands—elders that never left us? Coaxing us here,
to the base of our nation—E kuʻu kupunahine,
ʻauhea wale ʻoe?*

TONY ROBLES

CAREER DAY WITH A FILIPINO COWBOY FROM HAWAI'I

I'd landed in Hawai'i
With the silent thud
Of a coconut falling
From a tree

My father's wife
Was from the islands
So we packed up our things
And made the 2 thousand
Mile trip from San Francisco

It was tough
We lived in
Back of a house
Owned by my dad's
Mother and father-in-law

It was in the back
That he kept his
Janitorial equipment,
Imported from San Francisco

He had dreams
Of working for himself

Vacuums, mops, buckets,
Carpet shampoo machine,
A whole arsenal ready to take
The Hawai'i janitorial industry
By storm

I was a senior in high school
Who had ideas of being a
Radio DJ
And I'd pick mangoes from
The ground, bruises and all
(It was like gold)
As I walked to school with the
Smell of burning sugar cane
In my nostrils
And at school I was introduced
To pidgin and was told, eh brah,
You talk like one haole
(Which was true, I did talk like
A whiteboy compared to the locals)

And one day the school had
Career day, with professionals
From many fields talking about
The opportunities in a number
Of professions

One of them was a DJ
From a local radio
Station
(A country station)

He was a Filipino guy
Who stood no more than
5 foot 3
He wore a cowboy hat
With a huge feather
Sticking out

(Which made him look 5 foot 5)
He stood in front

Of us and began
Pacing across the floor
He spoke with an affected
Southern accent and moved
As if having ridden a horse for
A week or suffering from a bad
Case of hemorrhoids
And he said,
I work at a
Station, rot thar,
Pointing towards the
Back of him with his thumb

And rot thar
Is where I made
My mistakes
Like playing the record
At the wrong speed

And rot thar
Is where I got my
Experience

And he continued to
Talk about radio, this 5 foot
3 inch Filipino guy with an
Affected southern accent who
Moved with what appeared to
Be a very sore ass on career day

And I sat
there thinking to
myself: Eh bruddah, you
talk like one redneck

THE SNAIL HUNTER OF KAHALU‘U

25 April 2020

The woman who hunts snails with cooking tongs in her pajamas
was smoking a cigarette outside her town house this morning. A
long, thin cigarette. I asked if she'd injected bleach this morning.
"How long can we put up with this crap?" she asked the smoky air.
Still has her job, but expects a pay cut, and has a mortgage to pay.
No stimulus check yet, but she heard about someone who got hers a
year after she died. The snails are fewer; they come out in the rain.
The sister to Gerry, a fierce woman who walks bent at the waist,
told me, "a friend texted to say, this is just like Hitler." She's Jewish.
Their brother (Gerry says his education was a waste of their
father's money) watches Fox. "If he so much as texts me or calls me
or emails me, I told him, it's going in the trash. It's his job, she told
him, to make his wife smile, his kids smile, his grandkids—does
he want them to remember his hate? She's wearing a shirt with
PARIS on the front, a sketch of the Eiffel Tower. "It's criminal," her
husband Wally tells me as I continue up the hill with Lilith. Judy of
the lush garden says, "he's crazy, that one." Her roses were getting
smaller in their pots. Now they're bursting into bloom. And there's
a lotus coming, too. I looked around, thinking there was a Buddha
in her yard, but I must have misremembered.

SUSAN M. SCHULTZ

AMERICAN ANGER

8 August 2019

The white man who hates millennials, thinks that Hillary "is the corrupt one" (while claiming to not like Trump), and who walks a small, fluffy one-eyed dog named Rosie, crossed the street before Lilith and I got to him. I was walking toward Hui Iwa Street and he turned to walk in parallel. Then the yelling began, not from the corner this time, but from at least 50 feet away. "That's a stop sign! JACKASS!" he yelled at a woman in a blue Smartcar, who had turned right onto Hui Kelu. I considered suggesting that yelling doesn't help, but thought better of it. When Lilith and I got back closer to home, the man with two fluffy white dogs, Mochi and Manju, told me he and his family were almost killed at that intersection by a speeding, swerving, Acura. "And I could tell you which woman always runs that stop sign," he added.

SUSAN M. SCHULTZ

THE MAN DOWN THE HILL
6 January 2020

I knew better. I knew better than to say anything more than hello to the white-haired white man down the hill. He was walking his small one-eyed Rosie and I Lilith. I watched as Lilith sniffed Rosie, as she always does other dogs. He wished me a happy new year. I said something about the state of the world. "It's always been that way, and it always will be," he said. "I've been there and I know it." I asked what he knows, and his voice changed timbre, turning to a growl. "They're ignorant, the rag-heads or whatever you call them. They hate us because we are." I told him he's a racist and turned to continue my walk with Lilith.

SERENA NGAIO SIMMONS

OTHER PEOPLE

*Come **home***
*go **home***
*the only way to connect is by being at **home***

Then will you pay for my ticket?
Get me on a plane every time I need it?
Or will you
find the tree, teach me to carve and shape the waka
show me how we used to move between motu, glide with it,
hoe, hoe, hoe ara like Horouta with it
all the way back to Te Tairāwhiti, nei?

*You should learn the **reo***
*Kāo, kōrero i te **reo** Māori, girl*
*you can make time for the **reo**, no excuses*

So you spotting the fees for the lessons then?
Shot bro, you topping up my HOP card as well
since I am prolly bus-ing it to all these wānanga?
How about when I want to practice
will you practice with me? Or am I too teina for you?
Will you promise to hold me when matua shames me in the marae?
Get me a brand new, blackened tongue since mine is too bleached?

Blood
blood
blood

Yeah about that one, I don't remember
where I put mine, can I borrow yours, sis?
Can you show me again how deep I'm supposed to dig?
How much of the guts I need to show
and how to put them all back in again when done?
Will you send me the papers for the land after? For belonging?
Will this hurt my future children as badly as it hurt(s) their mother?

Ko Hikurangi te maunga
Ko Waiapu te awa
Ko Ngāti Porou te iwi

How often have you sent Uenuku just for me?
How can I smell your smoky morning all the way from Hawai'i?
When I finally make it up the maunga
will you hold the sun for me?
Why did it take me so long to open to you?
To see you in the sky, the street, music, my smile?
And how silly it'd be to ever let go after all that?

SERENA NGAIO SIMMONS

URBAN NATIVE

How do I tell all of them
those natural
healthy
good natives

ones with the nice sunsets on their lanai
that locally grown & sourced budget
no idea what it means to have the entire breath of a city
so imbedded in your everyday
not even the earth can fill you when you're ripped away from it

How do I tell them
that I fuck with sweet potato
but only when it's next to some cow?
That cheese on toast
or a bag of Doritos
is sometimes what I need after a hard day,
that mum & dad did the best they could
but as many days as she cooked,
mum also had to come through with the Happy Meal
because
either way,
I need to get fed

Will they believe me when I say
that I'm decolonized?
Every post or status they make having something to say
about a sustainable diet,

how the body is now rinsed thorough with sovereignty
I grew up at the bottom of the mountains, so this is the only way
I know,
but I was raised on the white man's sugar,
crave it
speak Mana Māori Motuhake in the same breath as
"yo can we stop at the Jack in the Box on the way home?"

Will they acknowledge my type of chain breaking?
See my resistance as valid?
I get restless in Kahaluʻu & during the middle of the night in
Glenfield
love waking up to the sunlight but need a couple of cars outside to
complete it

So from good to bad on the native scale
where do I sit?
Where do I get placed?
Sad half-blood with no taste for vegetables
or the stomach to live too far outta the city,
tell me again
how much time I'm shaving off my life
by "choosing" the taquitos at the 7-Eleven over a kale smoothie
how much more connected to my heritage I would be
gardening out in the kūmara patch instead of digging myself deeper
into Waikīkī and Chinatown's heartbeat

What do you say to each other when we aren't there?
Us urban natives
the ones who never got the forest hikes growing up
hauled off for a work day in the kalo patch,
used to a Whopper and fries

but have a hard time when our own food is put on the table

Those of us who were born and brought up away from the haukāinga
never taught our language,
the cousin who watches and can't sing along
spent our first night on a marae at 21
and knowing that no matter what,
we will always be considered some sort of "incomplete"
some sort of "half"
not enough

How much longer does it take for us to get there?
To become full like you?
When will my blood go from half-bleached
to ancestor brown?
What I would give
to be like centuries past,
the amount of salt cemented into my face from all the crying
imagine the muliwai I could make with it
how much of my later teenage years spent hating myself
for my skin
for my diet
for the way my body reacts whenever it's surrounded by trees
instead of buildings

I'm sorry
now that I'm older
I've become less good at trying to make you like me
wish I inherited farming and country living from my great
grandparents
but I got a different survival
out here on the margins,

recognize the value of growing up with family
but still hold the important lessons every adopted uncle and aunty
on the corner of Liliuʻokalani and Cleghorn gave me in my youth,
it'd be nice to have a vegetable now and then
but I know that what I do with my diet
has nothing in common with how the rest of this body gets liberated
I like that view over the bay at my sister Noa's house
but nothing beats the blending of the city lights as I drift off to
sleep

I'm afraid,
my living
my native
my decolonized
is something you're just gonna have to deal with

CORY KAMEHANAOKALĀ HOLT TAUM

PA PUAʻA A KĀNE

Pigpen of Kāne

One of the many ancient cultural sites on the cliff of the Koʻolau Mountains in Haʻikū Valley, which the 16-mile H3 highway currently runs through. This is where Kāne kept his prized hogs.

CORY KAMEHANAOKALĀ HOLT TAUM

WAʻA UKA

Aerosol and latex paint on invasive albizia tree

◀ This is my attempt to see through the eyes of our kūpuna and envision the waʻa when selecting the perfect tree. This was a site-specific installation at Hoʻoulu ʻĀina where they have repurposed this invasive wood to create canoes among other purposeful creations.

PUAʻA HIWA

Aerosol and latex paint on invasive albizia tree

A comment from a Kalihi kupuna regarding the destruction of a God stone when creating the Likelike Highway: "Only the sacrifice of a black pig, could undo this such great devastation."

CORY KAMEHANAOKALĀ HOLT TAUM

ROOT FEELING

Aerosol and acrylic paint on raw canvas

The juxtaposition of the "eyes" (nodes) of the ʻawa branches and the face of Kāne, the craving for the desired food of the Gods.

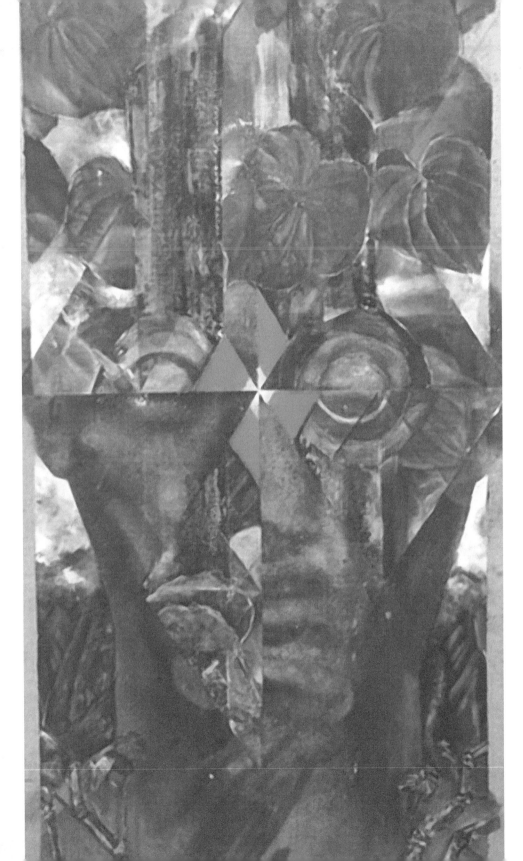

WE GO STAY COME

Thrust both hands into the moss
entrails of the earth, this island like a pig
in an imu. The transplant will not keep.

Speak how the earth grew iron
around our wrists, and we were left staring
only at the opened ground.

Clouded fish eyes blink in the night;
their gaze falls down on our bare necks.
Hope for a slate made of sand and waves.

And remember we left once, a long time ago.
I suppose it is only time until we go
again, into another leaving.

After all, everything washes out to sea.
Even the limp glow of streetlights
that moan "lament lament lament" tonight.

So we wait in partial penance, partial breath
until something comes crashing down, or creeping up
upon the place we lay our heads.

Hear the rain sweep the mountains the way a skirt
folds in the wind. Hear the mountains reply
with mist and smoke. Hear: they talk amongst themselves.

LIZ TENRAI

EDEN

I walk through Eden,
and it looks like someone's backyard.
There's a bleeding mango tree
and sour cherries and fuzzed tomatoes.

I walk through a land that belongs to others.
A black dog pads down the street, sniffing
rank weeds and trash cans.
No one told me there are starfruit here.

I do not know what it is to walk
my teeth into the slick insides of a persimmon
and chew in peace. There is no
land that loves me back.

What ethnicity is your mother?
Jesus next to me at the table,
the brownness of his hand in mine
no less than God's.

My mother waits in eternal patience
cross-legged in front of us.
We need to know what this hapa haole boy
is going to do to me.

OUT OF YOUR HOMELAND

I. The Yo-Yo Doll
if only I had the doll you made
in Queen's Hospital when I was six
you stitched through centers of calico-puckered circles
to stack arms and legs
you sewed on a yellow pom-pom for a face

when we came to pick you up
you sat in the backseat with me
the doll in your lap
I so admired it
me no like you said
why I asked
if Baban no make dis kine
no can come home
docta say I have to make so I make
you handed it to me
I held it uncertainly

no one told me why you went to the hospital
I asked about it 50 years later
Mom said you were *hearing voices*
so they gave you *electro-shock therapy*
knowing her mentality I could think of nothing to say

but I know in your homeland there's a name
for a woman of profundity
who is suddenly hearing voices

kami-daari refers to *illness*
on the path to becoming a priestess
there in your day a *yuta* would have done rituals
to carry you through
there would have been a forest to retreat to

II. In a Makawao Boutique
this doll leftover from Christmas stock
has calico-puckered circles sewn into arms and legs
its porcelain jester face probably painted
in a Chinese factory
I'd buy it on sale half-price
for the great granddaughter you've never seen
if it was some reminder of what you assembled to escape

but the polyester is stiff
it smells of chemicals
and your small shiny fingers
tattooed with ovals of green *hajichi*
have not worked their way over the flowery print

DELAINA THOMAS

THE CLEANER

I glance up as I enter Makawao Post Office
he's slightly stooped, wiping the counter

his skin is deep brown
his nose is hooked down the nostrils broad
the curve of his upper lip protrudes over the lower
the whites of his eyes are stark
against the hull of his cheekbones
his wavy hair is sprinkled white

you have a lot of Hawaiian blood I blurt out
he keeps wiping the grey Formica
are you pure Hawaiian? I ask
he looks up briefly *yuh* he replies
I knew it I say
my Uncle was pure Hawaiian
I hardly see anymore that look—the blood not mixed

I want to say *we should be wiping your counters*
and emptying your rubbish

he replaces the half-full bag with a new liner
I buy stamps from Mrs. Perreira
then turn asking *where are you from?*
Niʻihau he answers
I came here when I was five
but I didn't know the language so . . .

he motions through the air with the white rag
then he looks back down at the counter

I extend my hand as I leave
his grip is strong and warm
the glass door closes behind me
his voice those eyes
the mana of that humility
why so direly dropped among us
estranged
apologetic
a vanishing ember in the sand

two years later I recognize him
when I pick up LeiHina from her first kajukenbo lesson
at Eddie Tam Gym
he's standing at the door
Senior Grandmaster George Kaʻanana
16th Dan Black Belt

he doesn't remember me
thankfully
the assumptive
nīele lady

TRAVIS KAULULĀʻAU THOMPSON (TRAVIS T)

ALONE AT NIGHT

Alone at night on the beach
with a shovel and a bottle of whiskey
I dug through the shallow sand
until I broke through to the saltwater below
and took that as proof of life.
Proof, that I can still feel something.
Proof, that my heart still feels like the hills
when a thunderstorm rolls in
and pain rumbles into an ache
unpacking its bags and settling in
to the shelter of my bones.
Eventually the pain crashed
like a giant rogue wave upon the levees of my ribcage
and I screamed your name into the night
letting loose the house fire trapped in my throat
chasing away grief halfway down my spine.

Alone at night on the sea
I chummed the waters around my lifeboat
and beckoned sea monsters with eyes
colder than their blood.
They came to sing me siren songs
that leave weary sailors lost at sea.
Instead I grabbed tight onto their tail fins
and let them drag me beneath the surface to find you.
But I did not find you.
Because I did not drown.

Instead I learned to walk on water
and though I never found my sea legs
I stutter stepped my way into singing
melancholy love songs only the ocean can hear.
Sad songs that recall the rising tide
in your lungs.
How you were the sinking ship
no one could save.
And the ocean remembers.
Tells me that you had a voice the size of a barrier reef
and a laugh as big as Maui.

Alone at night, on Olomana,
I watched how the ʻāina carries the bodies of the broken
on its shoulders.
Reminding me that keeping my hurt
in a cage confined to the darkest corner of my mind
isn't called surviving,
just because the weight of its burden
bends your back like a rainbow to nowhere.
On Olomana, the trees whispered *"Kaululaʻau*
there is a koa forest growing in your spine,
and if you're too small to reach the top
you should never stop climbing."
So every night I went chasing the ghost of my father
through hurricane beaten coastlines of self
and my eyes never relented from storm-watch.

Alone at night
with a blank page and a pen
I found you between the lines.
So I made long distance phone calls

to the hole in my chest
where the last wheeze of a dying star
echoed through the universe
masked by the sound of songs
written in the coldness
of once warm memories.

TRAVIS KAULUĀʻAU THOMPSON (TRAVIS T)
AND KAMELE O PUʻUWEI DONALDSON

GO HOME, STAY HOME

What, bra, no can hear?!
What, bra, no like listen?!

I don't care if
round trip tickets to Honolulu were only one hundred and fifteen
dollars!
Nearly three million people are sick*
I don't care if
that Airbnb in Lanikai was only $20 a night!
Over two hundred thousand people are dead*
I don't care if
you think this global pandemic is just a hoax by "China and the
Democrats"
from Honolulu to New York City
two hundred million people are living under a government-imposed
stay-at-home order
So go home and stay home!

Tourists
Stay home!
College spring breakers
stay home
all non-essential workers

---

*Statistics reported by the Associated Press as of Monday, April 27, 2020,
were rounded up.

stay home

After all, uninvited outsiders invading Hawai'i
have always been non-essential
ever since Kānaka clubbed Captain Cook at Kealakekua Bay
outsiders invading Hawai'i has always been about colonization
has always been about capitalists' interests
has always been about stealing the land, kicking out Kānaka
and turning our 'āina into a parking lot and a playground
for those willing to pay the price of paradise
But Hawai'i is not your pandemic playground hideaway

Maybe you didn't hear when Governor Ige
encouraged tourists "not to travel to Hawai'i at this time"
Maybe you didn't hear when Mayor Caldwell
encouraged all new arrivals "to self-quarantine for 14 days"
So I am here to make sure you hear me loud and clear as I
encourage you, to go home and stay home!

Excuse me if I seem upset at the image of outsiders landing at
Honolulu airport during a global pandemic
Excuse me if I seem heated at the broadcast of Trump selling lies
about Lysol and UV floodlight enemas
Excuse me if I become triggered by CNN at the sight of dead people
in body bags stacked two deep on top of ice rinks

As a Kanaka I will tell you when outsiders invade Hawai'i
it is we that have died in the tens of thousands
matter of fact, we died in the hundreds of thousands
and we were not alone
For many Pacific Islanders throughout Oceania
the diseases of progress and travel are all too familiar to us:

1778, syphilis
1804, cholera
1820s, influenza
1839, mumps
1848, measles and whooping cough
1853, smallpox
1869, leprosy
2020, COVID-19

In less than a hundred years since the arrival of the West
nearly ninety percent of the native Hawaiian population was
make-die-dead
We chanted kanikau and danced the hula for the deceased
watching as our ʻohana cliff-jumped from Hāʻena Point
leaving footprints on the clouds at sunset
disappearing into the horizon with a green flash
joining our kūpuna
But no longer shall we only reserve our voices for grieving the dead
No longer shall we be silenced in the face of another
deadly pandemic
No longer shall we listen to "make nice and show aloha"

so Tourists
stay home!
College spring breakers
stay home
all uninvited outsiders and non-essential workers
stay home
and all racist capitalist imperialist globalizers and invaders
throughout Pasifika
GO HOME!
you and your kind are not wanted here

and we *"strongly encourage you"* to take your sicknesses back home
with you
and stay there

TRAVIS KAULUĀ'AU THOMPSON (TRAVIS T)
AND JESSE LIPMAN

THE ICE IS MELTING

Somewhere outside
city streets are blanketed in sheets of black ice
melting drip by drip
The atmosphere is changing

Somewhere outside
the snow is melting for the last time
streaming into currents, lost in storm drains, gutters of sickness
spilling back to a dead sea, resurrected in fraction of inches
inviting itself inland
disappearing beaches, birthing a great Pacific garbage patch twice
the size of Texas.
The fish are drowning in our undying plastic
Drips become ripples

Somewhere outside
climate refugees are running the from the tide chasing them to
higher ground
while we ignore dripping faucets, wash our hands with blind faith
in the market
flip carbon levels like condos
Morals never mix properly with money

The god we worship on our currency is the mirage of "progress"
answering us like the prayers of an atheist
Let thick breeze carry us like dry salt to vultures scavenging the
carcass of empire

Parasitic profiteers and bottom line puppeteers prostitute
our politics
so we are debtors to a system anchored like an oil rig to the
ocean's basin

Meanwhile
Real Global Terrorists decapitate rainforests.
Real Global Terrorists dam rivers for ransom, hold resources for
hostage
Real Global Terrorists frack the seafloor in search of oil, pave cities
over flood plains
Because Real Global Terrorists murder entire ecosystems.

So catch your breath beneath the underbelly of our over-consumption.
Cry me a merger when the rent's overdue.
Sing me a bedtime lullaby in a refugee tent.
"Alexa, wail me a blues song for gentrified graveyards
rising from the dead like landfills the size of mountains."

In the space between the Green New Deal and corporate interests
we've become non-recyclable waste:
Polar bears clinging to arctic glaciers the size of ice cubes,
sinking into extinction on Super Bowl Sunday.

Somewhere outside
the ice is melting
dripping tears through generations of our children's unborn children.
We are aborting gardens of sustenance
modifying the genes of our seeds to feed coarse throats.

We can't nurse Mother Earth back to health if our bad credit can't
afford her medical.

Father Time has foreseen every disaster brewing and is turning his
face backwards
All the cash money in the world will never be enough to hold back
the tide of our endgame
Hell will overheat before it freezes over
Soon, none of us will have anything to do with folded paper
but fan ourselves and pray for mercy
"Please Lord, help us save ourselves from a world on fire
bloated, from swallowing the sun."

LEE A. TONOUCHI

DA NORMALIZATION
OF WAR

One flier for da
Kāneʻohe Bay Air Show
at MCBH
says going get
da Navy Blue Angels,
da U.S. Navy's premier
flight demonstration team

along with
rides for da keiki!

On da bottom
it even
invites
schools
for schedule one visit.

In my mind
I imagine

what future

shows might include

Osprey Petting Zoo?

Throw da Grenade at da Milk Jugs?

Bumper Tanks?

And Dance Dance Wartime Revolution
where if you step one top
one landmine
your time is up.

HAWAI'I'S MOST DANGEROUS JOB

Hawai'i get all kine jobs
das abunai.

We get da regular
dangerous kine
like
Policeman
Fireman
Lifeguard.

But everyplace get dat kine.

What most people dunno
da scariest job in Hawai'i
stay
Landscaping Technician.

So sad li'dat.
I read 'em in da papah
two braddahs
wen get hurt
jus
from cutting grass.

See, these two guys
wuz jus regular
civilian contractors
trimming da weeds
at da
Mākua Military Reservation
when all of a sudden their
weed whacker
wen go bang
some unexploded ordnance.

Talk about
False crack, medivac
li'dat.

When asked for comment
on top dis tragedy
da Army spokesman
had dis for say,
"the person closer had more injury,
and the (other person) was a little bit farther away
and his injuries were less . . .
but they were both severe." [1]

I dunno, but sometimes when you say stuff
das jus so obvious
it jus comes out sounding
kinda dumb
and little bit insensitive too.

Like in da follow up article dat said,
"pending the completion of an investigation . . .
The Army said
it has stopped
all grass-cutting . . ." [2]

Fo' really?

[1] Cole, William. "2 Hurt in Makua Valley Explosion." *Honolulu Star-Advertiser.* 7 April 2015: B1, B3. Print.

[2] Cole, William. "Man in Ordnance Blast Still in Hospital." *Honolulu Star-Advertiser.* 10 April 2015: A23. Print.

LEE A. TONOUCHI

McGARRETT WOULD GO

When Steve McGarrett
went Afghanistan
and defeated
da Taliban
das when I thought
Hawaii Five-0
wen go
jump da shark.

But den
had one noddah one
wea McGarrett
had one building
blown up on top him
and somehow
he managed for survive,
escape,
and
save Danno too.

So den it's not
really so hard for believe
da recent episode wea
McGarrett saves
Hawai'i from
total nuclear annihilation.

Cuz in da show
da bad guys had for smuggle
one nuclear warhead
into our state.
But in real life
we just
let
all da nuclear weapons
come and go
through Pearl Harbor
and Local people,
ah we dunno what going on,
cuz nobody really asking,
but not like dey
would tell us
anyway.

Da only way
I know
is cuz one time
I wuz at one party
and my friend's friend's cousin
came straight from
his submarine,
so for make da conversation
I wen go ask him,
"I dunno if you allowed
for disclose such informations,
but I just curious,
does your vessel have
how shall we say 'em,

nuclear
capabilities?"

And all casual
he wuz all like, "Oh hell yeah!"
Like to him it wuz
da coolest ting in da world.

Das nice for know
I tinking
da fack dat get
one nuclear bomb
about two miles from
my house.

MAIKA'I TUBBS

ERASURE

2008

156″ × 72″ × 18″

audiocassette magnetic tape and
casings, wire

Erasure is a sculpture installation of
sixteen woven magnetic tape birds on
audiocassette tape casing branches that
tells the story of the extinct o'o bird.
Prized for its yellow feathers used in
traditional Native Hawaiian capes, the o'o
was eventually wiped out by animals and
diseases brought to the islands through
Western contact. Each bird unravels
into a pile below with a tiny magnet
attached to the end. The magnet, small
and unassuming like the first mosquito
brought to the islands, seems to slowly
erase the magnetic tape, leaving no data
behind. Without any o'o in present-day
Hawai'i to observe, the installation
provides the artist's imagined black-
and-white snapshot of what might have
been. *Erasure* speaks of extinction as a
byproduct of change and progress, using
the audiocassette tape as a symbol of a
technological castaway, an item deemed
unworthy in the natural selection of
tomorrow's newest inventions.

OLD MAN SPIDER

His name was Yomi. Yoh-mee. But us guys always used to
call him "Yummy." Old Man Yummy and the name made sense
because he used to always bring Ma and us all kinds of goodies,
fruits mostly. Brown cardboard boxes of bright, juicy tangerines,
plastic Ziploc bags of deeply colored lychee, and handfuls of unripe
mangos. We never liked that last one. They smelled too sour, filling
the kitchen with a pithy, bitter scent. Their sticky sap would
leave amber globs on the countertop that would get on our palms,
elbows, even our knees when we'd climb up there to steal pickled
plums from the glass jars Ma kept on the shelf over the sink. She
never let us eat them, not even if we begged. Those were our Popo's
plums and though a dead woman had no need for pickled fruit, we
would never tell Ma that.

We knew that he only brought over green mangos for Ma. We'd
seen how she'd slice them up, her mouth tight with anticipation.
And after she'd finish cutting them up, she would dip them in
shoyu sugar, those wide, flat pieces of pale-yellow flesh, still so
hard that they snapped under her teeth with a sound we could hear
from the next room over. In the days after Old Man Yummy had
come to visit, we'd often find clear containers of hard mango slices
submerged in dark liquid in the fridge.

Ma used to make us stand in the kitchen and thank him.

And we'd give him a flat, toneless chorus of, *Thank you, Unko Yummy.*

He was our neighbor. Our street ran up (or down, depends
how you want to take it) a slight slope and us guys being on the
bottom, Old Man Yummy's house loomed above us all our lives. A
dark house too large for one old man. Even then, we'd understood
that the fine dark wood and his pale painted roof set that house

apart. The fruit trees around it in his large backyard seemed to be perpetually heavy with food even when out of season. Our own house was always too small, packed to the brim with bodies and bodies, Ma's brothers and cousins, calabash and all, would cycle in and out. Our tin roof would shine embarrassingly in the sunlight at the bottom of our sloping cul-de-sac we called Grody Road. Something we probably heard from one of Ma's brothers and we mistakenly took it as fact.

Years down the line when we call it that at family parties, funerals, and weddings like that, our aunties and uncles sneer and ask us where we heard that. Did we really think that was the actual name of the street? What kind of road is named "Grody"? They'll laugh and joke and we marvel at how we can still feel like children though childhood is long past. How shame can make you feel young again. And part of us wants to protest, to explain ourselves. We just wanted to be like you. Didn't you know that? We wanted to talk like you, eat mangoes like you, and swallow back tears, eat our own rotten tongues, break our hearts before anyone else could, just like you did. We just wanted to be part of you.

Old Man Yummy kinda looked like a spider. We all thought so, and we didn't like it. He had these long, thin limbs all bent with age. His skin and what little fat he had that wasn't on his gut would hang from the bones of those spindly limbs. His bald head sat crooked on his sloping shoulders, so devoid of any fat and flesh that it looked more like a skull with skin pulled tightly over it. We'd grimace at the beading sweat on the back of that yellow skull. It would form like little pimples on his skin as he lugged his many treasures up the steep stairs in the back of the house that led directly into the kitchen.

And he had no teeth! Imagine our surprise the first time we'd seen him smile, all pink and fleshy. One of us might have even laughed when he'd peeled one of those tangerines and gnashed toothlessly at the tiny pieces that glistened like jewels with all that sweet juice.

He was funny lookin' and we tried once to ask Ma about it.

How come he look like that? Why he no mo teeth? How come he walk so funny?

And Ma would frown, tell us, *eh, you nieles! Who wen raise you fo talk like dat about yo unko?*

We don't give her the obvious answer to spare her feelings. She had been the one to raise us. And Old Man Yummy *did* walk funny. Even if Ma didn't agree with us, we knew she noticed. She'd watch him from the window over the sink that looked down on the back stairs as he hobbled down leaning heavily on the wobbly, termite-eaten railing. Just to make sure he made it down okay. A couple times she had gone out to help him, letting him lean on her.

We think Ma is the most beautiful woman in the world, the most benevolent. Her round belly, her dark face and all its beauty-mark constellations. We learn later that she is not beautiful. Her thighs are too soft, her face too round. There's no Disney princess that looked like Ma, no model or movie star with dark hula hair kept in a pile on the top of their head or wide, chubby hips. Beauty doesn't have a double chin so soft and plump to press little kisses on with mouths still sticky with the juice of many fruits. But secretly, we still believe in Ma's beauty long past the point that we should have learned to scorn it. We know she carries our family on her back. We've seen our uncles cycle through the house, bringing with them their sly, mean mouths, their many girlfriends smelling of freesia, plumeria, or even tiare but always underneath is the smell of acrid booze. They bring their friends with their hungry bellies and heavy hands and gobble up the fruits and other treats that Old Man Yummy had gifted us. The apple bananas so sweet and tangy, the bright, bitter jabongs, even Ma's mangoes fell victim to our uncles and their hunger.

But we can't say anything, we learn to hate the taste of our own tongues in our mouth, feel them rotting, dying as we keep quiet. And though we see the heartbreak on Ma's face, see it cloud the starry sky of her face, we can do nothing to clear it. We, with our twig arms and narrow shoulders. We, with our pookah teeth and stained, hand-me-down clothes. What could we do against hungry uncles? Maybe that's why we decide to treat the old man like we do, because we know we can beat him. Because we know, our uncles let us know, that you should never pick on someone your own size. Only fight someone you know you can win against, that you know is smaller, weaker; pick someone who loves you. So, we turn on the old man. We attack, jab in the way we know best. We talk story. Just amongst ourselves, we say nasty things about him.

He steals those fruits, you know.

It's a lie or at least we don't know if it's the truth. We can't remember which one of us said it but we remember how it made us feel, how it sparked to life our imaginations.

Only he eat da fruit in his yard. He give us all da stolen ones. So cheap that old spider!

We congregate in our Popo's room and chitter about Old Man Yummy. It was the only place we knew we'd be safe, the place we could keep our secrets. Though our Popo, our mother's mother, had died years before we'd even been born, Ma had kept her room untouched, the only thing she'd been able to keep safe from her brothers' greedy hands. But not ours.

When Ma is away at work, we sneak into Popo's room and rifle through things. It's the biggest room and sat at the front of the house. Though just as full and bursting at the seams with things that had long since lost their usefulness as the rest of their poor house, Popo's room had an untouched lifelessness that rendered it pristine. We'd learn soon that only the dead can be so clean.

The first time we'd dared to venture into this forbidden temple to a woman long dead, we'd been dazzled by the sheer luxury of the place. Popo had her own half bathroom, with pale green walls and pretty crystal faucets for the sink. Tiny glass bottles filled with strange smelling liquids were placed at random in white plastic trays that ran along the left side of the sink and many pill bottles still half-filled line the other side.

Pearl, the bottles read.

When we see her in black-and-white photos, a fair-faced, thin-eyed woman neither smiles nor blinks, we cannot help but think she looked the part of a Pearl. There's a portrait in a silver frame that sits at the center of the Pearl's dresser. In this tarnished cage is a small woman with a face like the moon, her dress is white, intricate and to look at it makes us ache in a way we cannot name but we know it innately. The man besides her, just as pale, is not our grandfather. His face is too thin. His face is too white, too clean and proud. In photos, our grandfather always casts his face to the dirt.

Popo's dresser is a mess of beauty and intrigue. Covered in crochet and lace doilies that may have been ivory once, more photos and other trinkets sit. We look through her jewelry and don't know that it is fake. We never get to see the plain box that's kept under her heavy bed, almost too large for the room, where she kept her jade pieces and a ring that she had once thought would be her wedding ring. In her closet, her clothes still remained. Most were worn and plain, clothes that we knew all too well but at the very back, hidden away were beautiful silk dress in bright colors and ornate designs. Blouses made of linen and cotton, long skirts made of fine material, and all of these were lightly perfumed. Powdery, floral, and nostalgic, these clothes smelled of something we had forgotten. We had never even met our Popo and yet we knew her smell.

It was here that we told our stories to each other. Here we forged the only weapons we could manage against the only enemy we could hope to conquer.

Old Man Yummy eat flies.

And we would see it. Our words would make it so. And the next time we'd see the old man with his fruits and treats, we would whisper amongst ourselves about the dark spots in his gums. These were all that was left of the flies in his house.

Old Spider kills dogs, shits standing up.

We'd surely seen him do it. We said it and it was so.

Old Spider killed someone for the mangoes he gives Ma! He's in love with her. NO! Old Yummy has no heart! He only gives us fruit cuz he like oof.

That's too far. We remember the cold touch of shame and how it made us shiver and turn our faces to the floor. We look around at one another, trying to figure out which one of us said it. We don't know. We can't tell. It came from nowhere; it came from someone else. It wasn't us. It was that old spider that put it in our heads, put it in our mouths. Skehbeh! Nasty, dirty spider. Old Man Yummy with his gnashing, pink mouth. We would make ourselves sick with the thought of Ma kissing those pale, thin lips the way she'd eat unripe mango slices. We could barely stomach it, the image of Ma so young and pretty, her face so sweet and soft. But our disgust made us feel strong, made us bold. We would never let it happen. We'd kill Old Spider before he'd ever get the chance.

The next time we see him, his bald skull shining with sweat, we are armed with empty bellies, our ears full of angry stories. When he gives us his gummy smile, we glare and sneer. Whenever Ma's is turned away, we make faces, stick tongue. Under our suspicious animosity, we see Old Man Yummy wilt. His smile wanes and we think we even see his limp worsen, favoring his right leg as he hobbles away. The sound of his uneven gait creaking down the kitchen stairs fills us more than any fruit or pickled plum could.

One of us had found a window in Popo's room that was high enough to see into Old Spider's house. It could only be reached by stacking ourselves on one another. We'd take turns peeking out at him from each other's shoulders. What we saw fueled us.

The old man's got tits! His saggy tits go past his opu!

We giggled at our mean-spirited gossip. Of course, we'd seen the suggestion of his sagging chest beneath the fine linen shirts he'd always wear. Expensive Aloha shirts paired with pressed slacks, proof of his wealth that we had come to resent so much. When we see him next, we show him our evil grins. Our snide smiles and pookah teeth. We could even see into his room. Laughed at his old frail body putting on his nice clothes in the hopes of impressing Ma. But we knew what was underneath. We had seen his old gut, his sagging flesh.

He shits himself. Watch. We see um tonight. His shitty bebadeez!

The first and last time we'd dared to spy at night, we feel strong. Our cruelty makes us bold. The memory of Old Man Yummy's faltering smile fortifies us. And we feel no fear sneaking through the house at night, stealing away into Popo's room under Ma's nose. We enter the room lit only by the moon pouring in from our secret window. Jan ken po decides who will be our eyes. The rest of us are too giddy to feel disappointed as we hoist our eyes up to see what fun we can make of Old Spider.

We see him moving, limping around his too-big house. Serves him right to have so much and need so little. When he comes into his room, we feel electric. We watch him remove his shirt to reveal the white wifebeater underneath and snicker at the sweat spots across his chest and under his pits. He removes his pants to reveal his clean white bebadeez. These sag too.

Saggy Old Yummy, we all whisper.

There's no shit on his bebadeez but we can make it up. We can all pretend it's what we saw. We were about to leave until our eyes catch something we can't ignore. His left leg. We'd never seen his legs and though the one we can see, his right leg, is as spindly and spidery as the rest of him it is the left one that makes us pause. It's wrong. Discolored and stiff. We'd seen him favoring his left leg often enough and we thought maybe the old spider's leg had gone rotten.

Rotten Sagging Spider.

But then, he leans forward. We think we can hear his back creaking with the effort as he reaches for his left leg. We imagine his long, crooked fingers and what they might be doing to his offending limb. What magic was he casting? What sinister plan was he hatching? Our imaginations run wild but still it falls short as after a few moments of fiddling, he curls back up and the leg just pops off. We are too stunned to react. All together, we hold our breath only to let it out in a chorus of wails when we watch his leg, cut off just below the knee, stretch and move. We scream at the blunted limb in our head. It is like we had all seen it and so we all feel the terror of its image.

The next time we hear his uneven creaking at the kitchen window, we are already overcome with the memory. Ma greets him at the kitchen door, takes his heavy gifts and welcomes him in. We all want to scatter but Ma would give us dirty lickens. She'd been severe since she'd found us all wailing in Popo's room, had turned our okoles bright red with the end of her longest bamboo rice paddle.

We don't feel strong anymore. We don't feel bold. When we catch sight of his left leg, we shrink. Old Spider's beat us. We hang back and try not to let Ma see the shame on our faces. But Old Spider's not done with us yet. He sees us, sees our fear, sees our shame and, almost as if he knows he's won, he smiles at us. It's the same gummy smile we'd seen every time before but the sight of that rounded, blunt mouth. The dark spots in his gums, we cannot contain our terror.

Spider!

We scream in his face.

Skehbeh! Rotten! Dirty!

We throw ourselves to the ground. We wail and swing our limbs about. We beat our heads where the image of the old man's blunted leg lives. We keep going, even after Ma raises her voice, even when our mouths go dry, even when the old spider scurries away. We don't care about Ma's rice paddle. We don't care about the fruit going rotten without our mouths to take them.

Old Man Yummy never comes back after that. We never hear his uneven gait under the kitchen window or the creak of the kitchen stairs. We never go into Popo's room again. We never dare to see the secret through the high window in her room. The fruit still appears in the kitchen. Tangerines used for juice, peaches and plums for pickling, bananas baked into bread that sticks in our throats and feels like sand in our mouth. We try to forget the sight we'd stolen that night. We try to forget the sinister gleam of his wet, pink gums as he smiled at us from the kitchen door. We try to forget he beat us.

We don't see him again for a while. We teach each other new stories and make up other games. We put away Old Spider, we've folded the memory of his gnashing mottled gums, his spider limbs like a moth-eaten linen and placed at the back of our minds. We've put away the memory magic until we see him, squatting beside the house, catching the shade cast by the wall he's leaning against. When we come upon him, we're struck by how little we feel when we see him sitting like a crumpled piece of paper in the shade. At his feet is an empty cardboard box, the slight smell of vegetal sweetness clinging to it and above his head, is the same window we'd spied him through all that time ago. From this side of the wall, our window looks ordinary, harmless.

When we approach, we see something like fear in his hooded eyes. We know the look, seen it traded amongst us too many times. His thin limbs tense up, ready to dash away should we spook like we had before. But we remain silent, watch him with cautious but curious eyes. In his hand is half an avocado, the flesh inside's been taken out and sliced then piled back into the empty skin. He'd been eating the pieces. We'd seen him push the soft, yellow-green pieces past his pale lips and lick his fingers clean. He watches us, careful not to smile. Careful not to move.

Give us some, Unko Yummy.

Hunger compels us to ask. Perhaps it was a hunger that compels him too, to give us his green bounty so easily. He offers the fruit, stretching out his hand, which we had once made into a claw, made into a fearful thing. Thin, crooked fingers unfurl to reveal just a hand, shaking and mottled with age spots. We pick at the chunks with our dirty fingers and marvel at the fat, sweet taste. Fine white sugar over avocado.

We pick the thing clean, lick our fingers for the taste. We'd eat the skin too if he'd let us, but he discards it down into his empty box and reaches into his pants pocket. He produces another avocado, still whole and still unripe. It is like a stone in our hands when he hands it to us. We pass it around as he nods and smiles, tells us to take it home. Though we give him no answer, no thanks, he continues to beam, that old gummy smile even as we run away, cradling our precious treasure.

The next day when we slice it open, we find the flesh too hard. It's dry and bitter but we eat it anyway. We swallow it down all the same and try to remember the fat, sweet taste of Yomi's avocado. Our mouths itch with the memory and the realization Old Spider's beat us again. 🕷

PERSONAL

I just one coocoo mahu
who like hook upp wit' you

So if you rock, rap, write,
publish, paint, paddle, parkour,
deejay, dance, design,
surf, snowboard, or skate,
you like go on one date, o' wot?

I not one slut!
Just like to look and act like one,
'cause ... well, it's fun, cuzz!

so if you t'ink you can
whoa man handle
this punkee
kinda funkay
small-kine chunky,
pot junkie fre-male,

sen' her an email
wit' some pics
of your face, dicks, and/or feet
den maybe we could meet
fo' some sweet tricks,
my treat.

Oh, an' like da song say:
Local Boys No Ka Oi
K?!

MAHEALANI PEREZ WENDT

NA WAI EA,
THE FREED WATERS

A Story of the People of Koʻolau Moku, Maui Hikina

1. *Mahiʻai Kalo, Taro Farmer*

All his life loving earth
  a living harrow waist deep in mud
planting tilling trenching shoveling plowing
  mud to field, gravel to path, stones to bank
yoked no less than animal to plow
  a year of this then *huki ʻai*, harvest
shouldering the heavy bags
  heaving lifting hauling slogging
through acres of taro fields
  ancient footpaths fragile *ʻauwai* wetlands
swollen feet hands torqued elbows knees
  pestilences infestations droughts
year after year, year after year
  for love of family love of ancestors
love of the Elder Brother
  for love of *Hāloa.*

2. *Loʻi Kalo, Taro Fields*

As far as eye could see their green hearts
  were laid bare under rains
that never ceased falling a much aggrieved sun
  the dim glint of it through upstart clouds
but always the rains and he was glad for the gods'
  beneficence and the harbingers who coaxed

sunlight's bright threads the 'auku'u, herons hovering
      then ensconced in pools
of watery green expanse their emanations of light
      vectoring the same paths trod
the same earth the same ancient waterways
      the ancestors walked he regarded the plants
hungrily the same green ones whose presentiments
      were his Elder Brother *Hāloanakalaukapalili*
vivified who was born of the gods
      Wākea and *Ho'ohōkūkalani* their union
a conflagration of heaven and brightening stars
      their firstborn, the Elder Brother
stillborn buried Ho'ohōkūkalani's tears unceasing
      until the quickening
shimmer of green in graven earth
      the unfurling leaves
and the risen Hāloanakalaukapalili
      progenitor
his offspring the stalwart green-hearted ones
      who followed growing up
out of the same earth again and again
      he called them *koa*, warriors
as they hoisted their green banners
      forming leaf arbors under sun's radiance
their stems rooted deep their arbors
      protecting parents, grandparents, the corm, *mākua*
protecting children grandchildren, *'ohā*, the offshoots
      succoring cradling them
millennia of generations turning returning
      e huli, e huli, e huli ho'i, the ancestors called
their names auspicious names naming
      their offspring in dreams

through keen observations
  hō'ailona, signs
close attentions to minutiae of corm
  stem petiole rhizome
shimmering sun wind
  sea clouds and earth
cradle of the hallowed ancestors
  and the risen Hāloa
give us the right names the *mākua* prayed
  dispatched their entreaties released them
mana 'ulu, mana 'ōpelu, mana weo,
  mana uliuli, mana 'ula'ula, moi, piko,
lehua, ha'akea, hapa hapapū
  were names given
and many more all his life
  he knew and never forgot
their names
  sacred from the first
they were the names of the generations
  of his Elder Brother
they were the names of his family
  they were the names of kalo.

3. Maka'ala, Be Vigilant

Elena his grandmother James and Samson
  the grandfathers who brought him to the gods
he followed along the ancient paths
  of well-tended fields
the rows of plants who were offshoots
  of his Elder Brother green sentinels
as far as eye could see
  he sloshed through the maze of waterways

the irreproachable fretwork of ancestors
      arrayed he heard
their songs prayers incantations
      traceries of winds waters ocean
he heard *Pahulena* the grandmother's birthplace
      she said her birthplace name
and motioned toward a dense growth
      of *'ōlena* and the tall stand of *niu*
where *'ehu kai* breezes warmed
      the wide river mouth churning
above reddish brown sheen of seaweed *limu kohu*
      spawning place of *āholehole, moi, 'anae,*
pāpio, 'o'opu, hīhīwai, po'opa'a
      'opihi, wana, hā'uke'uke, 'a'ama
he remembered stories fishing canoes divers their nets
      the surround of *akule, halalū,* mishaps at sea
the *kilo i'a*, fish spotter's lair high above the *kāheka*
      the first catch offered there at the *ahu*
he remembered his grandmother's warning
      maka'ala and that after the bosses came
aia nō iā ha'i nā 'āina o mākou she said
      other men have our lands
then her words went dry
      and Pahulena was no more.

4. *Waimaka, Tears*

There are hidden places
      where the high waters fall
in rainbowed silence
      sucked in through igneous stone
pulsing the columnar dikes
      of earth's vast waterworks

spilling over soul's sacred edge
       Elena's tears Elena's tears.

5. Naʻaupō, Ones Devoid of Light

From sea dregs the onslaught winds
       its shifting stars, the detritus tides
carry dark strangers
       under cover of night
stealthy ones of fervent prayers
       and exhortations Holy Father
bring us safely to the village
       Pahulena in the distance
grant us safe conduct
       in our sacred mission
to save the unbelievers
       for Your greater glory
Amen.
       he malihini lākou no ka ʻāina ʻē
ka ʻāina wai huna no Kāne
       strangers they come
to this land of hidden waters
       belonging to Kāne
ghosts grey as gunmetal
       intractable as cannons
sulphurous gunpowder flashes
       their lodestars
at artillery's first report
       the stalwart sons and daughters of Hāloa
rout the shadowy ones
       but from dregs of darkness
there is no surcease
       wave upon unending wave

commend ravening spirits
       to the tasks set before them
conversions appropriations
       decimations subjugations
as has been foretold
       in their writs
they look upon Hāloa's people
       as pitiable idolaters unclean ones
who must brought to the One God
       and called to atone
from the lost souls' darkness withal
       a Savior shall lead them
their dark paths made light
       the Savior's blood sacrifice
upon Golgotha's mouldering cross
       their lamp of redemption
na'aupō look with dismay
       upon the god Lono's handiwork
his raft of green mountains
       his canopies of forest
they judge these iniquity
       evil fruit of indolence
an affront and mortification
       to industry
they are disdainful
       of Kāne, his Living Waters
flowering to sea
       abased are the natives
of this extravagant land
       upon their stolid ramparts
na'aupō recite oaths
       their kingdom come

their will be done
      they issue the edicts
dispatch the cadres
      to bulldoze the lands
build fantastic scaffolding
      engineering marvels, masterworks
for excavation of the high mountains
      extraction of waters
to bring the vile gods low
      to siphon off the lifeblood
from the green realms
      of the Elder Brother
the brooding altars are abandoned
      the disconsolate moon holds no sway
as the waters are wastreled
      the fate of an unrighteous people
turned in dark hands
      through a marvel of gravity flow
the waters are extricated
      ho‘ohemahema i ‘ō i ‘ane‘i
dug here, trenched there
      tunneled here, siphoned there
the uplands turned into wallows
      ‘ino ihu pua‘a
for dirty snouted pigs
      loosed upon the land
rooting here looting there
      through gross machinations
the sacred is harried in ungodly ways
      ditches pipes channels
tunnels siphons flumes
      aqueducts intakes funnels

dark grasping hands
        leering lewd imaginings
broad hillsides of waving cane
        the far distant and arid plains
prolific with cane tassels under brightening sun
        all of this has been foretold
all has been readied, all paths cleared
        the export tariffs have been lifted
foreign labor contracts signed
        the people's protestations—
the devil take them!
        the necessary approvals have been given
government officials are aboard
        the false idols *Kū, Kāne, Lono,*
Kanaloa a me nā akua apau
        banished to the greater glory
of Almighty God!

6. *The Fisher of Men*

From high promontories
        elevated stations of the cross
the bosses offer prayers
        for the blessing of verdant lands
mahiʻai in the fields
        lawaiʻa at the nets
and there are remembrances
        vague recollections
of One Other
        a Fisher of Men who once led them
who fed multitudes
        with few fish and loaves
the bosses remonstrate with themselves

as the tableau of *kua'āina*
unfolds in the lowlands
a childlike people easily duped
to be cajoled lured away
or forcibly removed
from the greening hills
what do they know these unwitting
of the true faith, divine purpose
the higher reckonings
of true believers
little do they know
of theft treachery genocide
deception stealth coercion
the idolaters must be readied
for the benefactions of civilization
na'aupō are filled with saccharine thoughts
of panoramic cane
the lands' expeditious acquisition
a foregone conclusion
the unrighteous ones' swift conversion
to a penitent upright people
the gift of civilization
a bargain more than fair
promised by the One God
who from the time of Adam
conferred to His true believers
dominion over the world
these truths being self-evident
the bosses are feverish
with thoughts of unholy war
upon *nā kua'āina* the people, their gods.

7. Naming the Waters

I ka wao nahele
> in the god-realms of *Koʻolau*

ka ʻĀina i ka Wai a Kāne
> the lands of the waters of Kāne

the sons and daughters of Hāloa
> named the waters:

where the long waters fell seaward
> ravishing black stones

where the eyes smarted from backspray
> and in dark depths like stars

the seed pearl oysters
> their faint songs could be heard

the name *Makapipi* was given;
> where *wī, hīhīwai* shells

migrated upstream and down;
> where *wī* groves

grew as thickets
> seeding the lands

where *wī* wind sounds were heard
> the name *Hanawī* was given;

where the waters scudded cloud-like
> as though firmament

where a red sheen was seen above
> signifying the presence of Sacred Ones

the name *Kaʻaʻula* was given;
> where the *moʻo* goddess

was well-pleased
> and smiled at her own reflection

in the shadow waters
> the name *Waiaʻaka* was given;

where limestone beds

of ʻākoʻakoʻa formed
and the ʻulu maika stones were shaped
    the name Paʻakea was given;
the narrow-necked gourds
    for water-carrying
gave Waiohue its name;
    ravenous Kamapuaʻa
the pig god
    his stampeding hordes
gave Puaʻakaʻa its name;
    where wauke was kneaded
to kapa of fine transparency
    stained with ʻākala berries
for a red birth gift
    Kōpiliʻula was the name given;
where two waters converged
    and ʻoʻopu scaled waterfalls
where Pele's sister the sorceress
    Kapōmaʻilele removed her genitals
sent them flying to thwart
    the rutting pig god Kamapuaʻa
his lust for Pele
    Wailua-Iki was the name given;
where Kāne-i-ka-Pahu-Wai
    Kāne of the Great Water Source
where he was seen in the heavenly clouds
    in the verdant mountainward ridges
where he was seen in the red-tinged rainbow
    where he was rain, lightning flashes
where he slept in the glowing light
    where his great heart was heard
in the thundering waterfalls

cascading stones quaking corals
where kalo was planted along the high ridges
        where it was planted in the wide valleys
where it was planted inland of the teeming shores
        kaulana nā ʻāina kalo
a nā hoaʻāina
        where famous were the kalo lands
and the people who cultivated them
        Wailua-Nui was the name given;
where the gods *Kāne* and *Kanaloa*
        refreshed themselves in springs
near groves of red and yellow lehua
        ʻŌhiʻa was the name given;
where the stout-stemmed olonā grew
        where in frigid waters the strands
were immersed cured
        braided into fine white cordage
for canoe lashings, fishing lines, nets
        where it was plaited
for chiefly raiment *ʻahu ʻula,*
        kāhili, lei, mahiole
where the stout-stemmed *olonā* grew
        Waianu was the name given;
where fine-grained *milo*
        were shade trees for the old chiefs
where windstorms incised the heartwood
        the omens carved into god likenesses
made into canoe paddles, serving bowls,
        implements for planting
where prolific headwaters
        were called *moana*
the name *Waiokamilo* was given;

where *mai'a* was food curative unguent
where its broad-leaf canopies
    were rain-coverings, enclosures
where spring waters bubbled up
    through igneous cinder, *'ākeke*
the name *Pālauhulu* was given;
    sentience along the high ridges
an exhilaration of climbing, of mounting
    gave *Pi'ina'au* its name;
where thundering rains
    poured down hollows caves ravines
where the tumult echoed down ridges
    sidewise along boulder-strewn sea cliffs
where earth shuddered and heaved
    with *nū* sounds
where great schools of fish hearkened
    where the torrents narrowed
Nū'āilua was the name given;
    where the torrents were made wide
Honomanū was the name given;
    where *hāpu'u, 'amau'u, hala, 'ohe,*
niu, loulu, kī, halapepe, 'ulu
    where *māmaki, 'iliahi, wiliwili,*
koa, palapalai, pala'ā
    where *kukui, hau, milo, kamani, 'awa*
where cherished forest plants grew
    the name *Punalau* was given;
where kapa-beating logs were harvested
    the black and red berries
strained for dyes
    the name *Kōlea* was given;
where a glowing light appeared

above the ridgeline
signifying the presence of Kāne
the name *Haipua'ena* was given;
where in cold springs
ali'i wāhine bathed
the name *Waiakamō'ī* was given;
where the ali'i wāhine ran
to the flat hiding stone
where she found refuge
from the pig god Kamapua'a
the name *Wahinepe'e* was given;
no ka mea, he mau inoa akua lākou
e ola nō lākou a pau.
in the god-inspired naming
the people remembered
because they remembered
the waters lived.

8. Ko'olau, The Windward Cliffs

All night
and for endless days like ghost canoes
at full sail under brightening moon
the billowing *'Ī'ale'ale* winds sweep across
Ko'olau mountain seacliffs
over razor-edged ridges valleys
with thunderous bursts exhalations
obscurations of light
the spectral crew worrying each blade leaf
branch with roaring cascades waterfalls
avalanches rockslides incessant rains
it is the season of *ho'oilo*
ho'īloli ke kai, the sea rages

the god Kanaloa furious his seamounts shaking
he hurls himself against seacliffs
    sending *'a'ama* scuttling over the reefs
shoals corals the staid seaweed
    limu wāwae'iole, limu manauea, limu 'ele'ele,
limu kohu, limu huluhulu waena
    their swaying frondescences under frothy waves
in the uplands kalo
    revel in watery pools
rainbows bead on the leaf-green
    arbors of scintillate light
refractions mirrored prisms riven
    by *Kāne-i-ka-Wai-Ola*
Kāne takes the form of a night owl
    he thrusts his wings and talons
disarming his enemies
    Kāne god of the living waters
walks abroad with Lono
    scion of water, scion of land together
summoning forth the sacred springs *'Oiana!*
    waters gush forth out of earth
the living waters of Kāne coursing to sea.

At the author's request, certain Hawaiian words have been italicized because to her,
they are beautiful and special.

STARSHIP AHUPUAʻA

This concept illustration was created for a STEAM coding and mural camp that was developed in partnership with Twiddle Productions Inc. The program's story imagines a future reality where the traditional concept of the ahupuaʻa system has been extended upward to include the heavens and stars. The floating islands or "moku ships" are adapted to exist in harmony with the resources and weather patterns around them. The following photos are from the UH Maui Center for Computer Learning where we painted the mural with the help of the students.

CONTRIBUTORS

Mark K. Anderson is a resident of Honolulu, Hawai'i.

An educator, **Amalia B. Bueno** is an award-winning poet and writer who is pursuing a PhD in English at the University of Hawai'i at Mānoa. "Perla and Her Lovely Barbie" appeared in *Growing Up Filipino II* (Philippine American Literary House 2010) and in the *Pinay Special Issue* (*Tayo Literary Magazine* 2017). Her poetry chapbook *Home Remedies* was published by Finishing Line Press in 2015.

Kamele o pu'uwai Donaldson was raised in the Pacific Northwest as a Kanaka in diaspora. She currently attends the University of Hawai'i at Mānoa, where she is currently pursuing her Bachelor's degree in 'Ōlelo Hawai'i. She began performing her spoken word poetry in front of audiences all across O'ahu in January 2020 and is a regular contributor to the Honolulu spoken word poetry community.

Ava Fedorov is a Honolulu-based visual artist, writer, activist, and educator originally from a remote region of Upstate New York. With a background that also includes design and film, Ava pulls from all realms of her creative knowledge to create immersive art experiences that blur the lines of genre. Her work has been exhibited, collected, and published internationally and she has been honored to collaborate with artists and art institutions across the world. Ava teaches studio art at Hawai'i Pacific University and is the founder and president of CICADA <cicadaartists.org>, an organization committed to amplifying the creative response to environmental justice and the climate crisis.

Allison E. Francis, PhD, is a Professor of English and Discipline Coordinator at Chaminade University of Honolulu who teaches and publishes scholarship in fields that include 19th Century African American and Caribbean Women's Literature, Victorian Literature, Scottish Literature, Theatre and Poetry, Vodou in Haiti, and Women's Fantasy Literature. She is also an actor, director, and performance poet. Francis presented a poetic Zoom event, "Mulatta—Not So Tragic," with poet-activist Karla Brundage, and they are collaborating on the publication of two volumes of *renshi* poetry. Francis archived her short play *Chocolate Cake,* commemorating George Floyd's death, to The Breath Project 2020.

Tom Gammarino is author of the novels *King of the Worlds: The Lost Years of Dylan Green* (2016) and *Big in Japan: A Hungry Ghost Story* (2009), and the novella *Jellyfish Dreams* (2012). Recent shorter works have appeared in *Tahoma Literary Review, Hawai'i Pacific Review, Entropy, The Writer*, and *American Short Fiction*. He received the 2013 Elliot Cades Award for Literature and teaches English at Punahou School.

Joanna Gordon is a writer and educator from the gentrified swamplands of East Honolulu. She graduated from the University of Hawai'i at Mānoa with a degree in English and completed a Masters in Fine Arts at Western Washington University. Her poems and prose have been published with *The Shore, Cherry Tree, The Tenderness Project, Nimrod International Journal*, and more. She has performed across national stages and participated in many full-length spoken word productions. She is interested in discussions of white privilege, diaspora, trauma, and tenderness. In her spare time, Joanna enjoys scalding cups of coffee, hiking, bright lipstick, and the company of great friends.

Sue Patricia Haglund, a Dule poet and scholar native of Panama, currently lives in 'Ewa Beach. She received her doctorate from the Department of Political Science at the University of Hawai'i at Mānoa. She has published in *Intensions Journal*, the first anthology of Dule poetry, *Antología de Poetas Kunas* (Panama, 2015), *Latinos Studies*, and *North Dakota Quarterly*.

Illnomadic: See **Navid Najafi**

Ann Inoshita was born and raised on O'ahu. She published a collection of poems, *Mānoa Stream* (Kahuaomānoa Press), and co-authored *No Choice but to Follow* and *What We Must Remember*, linked poetry (*renshi*) books (Bamboo Ridge Press). Her short play, *Wea I Stay: A Play in Hawai'i*, was included in *The Statehood Project* performed by Kumu Kahua Theatre and published by Fat Ulu Productions. Her creative works have been anthologized widely in local, national, and international journals. Her poem "TV" (written in Hawai'i Creole English, Pidgin) was published in *Reel Verse: Poems About the Movies* (Penguin Random House). "Red Banana in da First Grade" was first published in *Mānoa Stream* (Kahuaomānoa Press). She teaches at Leeward Community College.

Kristiana Kahakauwila is a hapa writer of kanaka maoli, German, and Norwegian descent. Her first book, *This is Paradise: Stories* (Hogarth 2013), takes as its heart the people and landscapes of contemporary Hawai'i. She has taught at Western Washington University and the Institute of American Indian Arts, and now is in the English Department at the University of Hawai'i at Mānoa. Kristiana is currently at work on a historical novel set on the island of Maui.

Juliet S. Kono: I've lived in Honolulu for many years, but have never appreciated the beauty of our islands and the goodwill of our people as much as in these times.

Jim Kraus lives in on O'ahu. His recent poetry has appeared in *Kinalamten Gi Pasifiku Anthology* (Guam), *The Cape Rock, Neologism, Voices de la Luna, Paragon Journal, Hawai'i Pacific Review*, and elsewhere. He is Professor of English at Chaminade University, where he teaches creative writing, environmental literature, and surf studies. He also edits *Chaminade Literary Review*. He enjoys swimming, surfing, visiting art galleries and museums, and reading contemporary poetry.

Kapena M. Landgraf: I grew up in the towns of Pepe'ekeo and Pāpa'ikou, later moving to Wainaku, Pana'ewa, and finally settling in Kaūmana where my parents live to this day. I moved to Honolulu in 2006 to pursue creative writing at the University of Hawai'i at Mānoa. I lectured there for several years after completing my studies. In 2018, I returned to Hilo to teach English at Hawai'i Community College. I'm glad to be back in my community again, teaching, learning, and writing among the sounds of the Hilo rain. My work is a navigation of self; a personal journey in rediscovering ancestry, place, and (hi)story.

Christina N. Lee is an English MA student with a creative writing focus at the University of Hawai'i at Mānoa. As a Korean American born and raised in Hawai'i, her poetry and prose are inspired by the landscape of Honolulu, immigration, culture, identity, loss, and mental health. Her writing integrates Korean folk songs and explores through language, the idea of being bi-cultural in Hawai'i.

Lanning C. Lee, born in Honolulu, earned his BA and PhD at the UH Mānoa, and his MA at the University of Wisconsin. One of the first six PhD candidates in English at UHM in 1987, he authored the first dissertation of creative writing. He's published two books of poetry, and his memoir, *From Point A to C to Y to B, a Sentimental Journey Through Hawai'i and Wisconsin*, came out recently. A collection of Hawai'i sonnets, a collection of Hawai'i short stories, and his second memoir will be published shortly. His first in a series of nine Honolulu crime adventures will appear soon in serial form. All are or will be on Amazon. Follow his daily writing blog, LanningLee.com.

Vanessa Lee-Miller, a poet, playwright and freelance journalist, was born and raised in Hilo, Hawai'i, where she still keeps one lū'au foot firmly planted on her 'ohana's kuleana. The other lū'au foot often travels to perform at literary events where the public's curiosity to hear Hawaiian in verse or drama has taken her to venues covering working-class pubs to the British Library and Pembroke College, Oxford. Often identified as a Hawaiian language activist, she describes her decades-long struggle to keep 'ōlelo Hawai'i alive as essential to preserving our culture: "The 'ōlelo is the place where its soul thrives."

R. Zamora Linmark was born in Manila and grew up and was educated in Honolulu. He is currently the Writer-in-Residence at Phillips Academy in Andover, Massachusetts, where he holds the Roger F. Murray Chair in Creative Writing. "National Crisis" could not have been written without wet market-based viruses, dangerous dictators (redundant?) and wanna-be presidents, endangered pangolins, and this crazy world and its even crazier, in-denial, degenerating denizens.

Jesse Lipman is the middle voice in a multi-generational family of poets. He's been performing spoken word, organizing poetry events, and publishing poetry in Hawai'i since 1999. These days you will find him colluding with the HI Poets Society, bringing people together around food in his work with Kokua Kalihi Valley and continuing to parent his almost grown kids a little more than they want.

Darrell H. Y. Lum used to edit *Bamboo Ridge* long time ago. Nowadays he write anykine and try make da editors laugh.

Native Hawaiian artist **Nanea Lum** is a University of Hawai'i at Mānoa Department of Art and Art History MFA (2021) and BFA (2014), an Excellence in Painting Awarded Artist, and 2013 Yoko Radke Awarded Artist for Excellence in Figurative Art. A POW! WOW! HAWAII! artist and Aupuni Space resident, she received the 2018 John Young Scholarship award and the Graduate Dean's Scholarship in the Masters' study of Painting. She is the current coordinator of the Hawai'i Arts Alliance Creative Network, which advocates for and supports artists who are permanent residents of the Hawaiian Islands. Nanea's areas of specialization include Hawaiian traditional craft techniques and art pedagogy involving place-based learning and indigenous knowledge.

Wing Tek Lum is a Honolulu businessman and poet. Bamboo Ridge Press published his two collections of poetry, *Expounding the Doubtful Points* (1987) and *The Nanjing Massacre: Poems* (2012).

Prana Joy Mandoe was born and raised in Hāmākualoa, Maui, where she learned to clean the water filter on a one-inch pipe in a dam that diverted Mokupapa Stream. She wanted the water to run in the streambed! Her love of the ʻāina led her to the Hawaiian community—an incredible teacher. In her own way, Prana has worked to support that community, teaching for social justice in Hawaiian-focused schools, raising children, and, in 2019, taking part in the movement to protect Mauna Kea and her waters from further development. "Four For Water" rises from these experiences.

From Maui, **Brandy Nālani McDougall** is the author of a poetry collection, *The Salt-Wind, Ka Makani Paʻakai* (2008), the co-founder of Ala Press, and the co-star of a poetry album, *Undercurrent* (2011). Her book *Finding Meaning: Kaona and Contemporary Hawaiian Literature* (University of Arizona Press, 2016) is the first extensive study of contemporary Hawaiian literature and the winner of the Beatrice Medicine Award. She is an Associate Professor of American Studies (specializing in Indigenous studies) at UH Mānoa. The poems published in this issue are part of her second poetry collection, *ʻĀina Hānau / Birth Lands*, which will be published in 2022.

Jonathon Medeiros has been teaching and learning about Language Arts and rhetoric for 15 years with students on Kauaʻi. He frequently writes about education policy and is the former director of the Kauaʻi Teacher Fellowship. Jonathon enjoys building things, surfing, and spending time with his wife and daughters. He believes in teaching his students that if you change all of your mistakes and regrets, you'd erase yourself. In his classes, he and students examine life with curiosity, learn, and cultivate empathy. He is currently working on a collection of essays, a full-length collection of poems from his family's daily writing practice during the global pandemic, and a journal about his days in the ocean. Follow him on Twitter - @jonmedeiros or at jonathonmedeiros.com

Shareen K. Murayama is a Japanese American, Okinawan American poet and educator. She has degrees from OSU-Cascades and the University of Hawaiʻi at Mānoa. She's a 2021 Best Microfiction winner as well as a poetry reader for *The Adroit Journal*. She promotes students' voices through a poetry club called the Po' Heads, spends her days as a surfing poet, and her evenings with her dog named Squid. Her art is published or forthcoming in *The Margins*, *MORIA*, *Juked*, *Bamboo Ridge*, *Puerto del Sol*, and elsewhere. You can find her on IG & Twitter @ambusypoeming.

Navid Najafi aka **Illnomadic** is a founding member of local conscious rap collective, the Super Groupers, and a two-time Nā Hōkū Hanohano Hip Hop Album of the Year award winner. Born in Tehran, Iran, and raised in New York, he found home when he moved to Hawaiʻi after high school. Aligned with core Hawaiian values of Aloha ʻĀina, he has become an active artist, organizer, teacher, mentor, and volunteer in the community. His style is activated hip-hop with lyrics that explore themes of migration, culture, solidarity, and home. Navid is currently the Learning Programs Coordinator at the Shangri La Museum of Islamic Art, Culture and Design and co-founder and administrator/artist for Soundshop, a hip-hop education workshop series at the Honolulu Museum of Art.

Artist **Matthew Kawika Ortiz**, from Lāʻie, Oʻahu, draws upon Hawaiian values and concepts to present them in a contemporary visual context. With a conscious attention to detail, Ortiz seeks to create work that invites viewers to imagine alternative realities to our current society and environment. He is interested in melding elements of the natural world with ideas of technology (both modern and ancestral), to create narratives around Mālama ʻĀina values. The theme of water or wai frequently appears in his work and he and his wife **Roxanne** form the artist duo **Wooden Wave**, best known for its signature sustainable treehouse murals.

Mark Panek has worked for two decades building a steady career as a third-tier state college writing instructor. He lives with his wife Noriko and son Kensuke in Hilo, where he as been a reliable member of the University of Hawaiʻi English Department since 2004.

Christy Passion is a critical care nurse and award-winning poet, author of *Still Out of Place*, and co-author of *No Choice but to Follow* and *What We Must Remember*. Her work recently appeared in *When the Light of the World Was Subdued, Our Songs Came Through: A Norton Anthology of Native Nations Poetry*, edited by Joy Harjo, the 23rd Poet Laureate of the United States.

Elmer Omar Pizo: Author, *Leaving Our Shadows Behind Us*, published by Bamboo Ridge Press in April 2019.

Born on Oʻahu, **Sean Rodrigues Pope** grew up in Maunawili and Kaʻōhao. His

Portuguese roots go back seven generations to the Hāmākua coast. He's the original drummer for Poi Dog Pondering, has lived and traveled extensively abroad and currently resides between Cologne, Germany and Detroit, where he is restoring a historic building.

Hōkūlani Rivera is a Kanaka woman from Pauoa Valley, Oʻahu. Due to the intergenerational impacts colonization has had on her family, she draws inspiration for her poetry from those who reside in her blood, but not her memory. Her piece in this collection, "E Hina," was specifically inspired by the recent discovery of her great-grandmother's name through archival research. When Hōkūlani is not writing, she is working as an AmeriCorps VISTA, a curriculum consultant for FEMA, a student at UH Mānoa, and a council member for the Climate Adaptation & Mitigation Program Fostering Indigenous Relationships and Education (CAMPFIRE) Council.

Tony Robles, the "People's Poet," born and raised in San Francisco. Graduated Waipahu High School in 1982. Still remembers the fried noodles from the manapua truck and Zippy's fried chicken. Author of two collections of poetry/short stories, *Cool Don't Live Here No More—A letter to San Francisco* and *Fingerprints of a Hunger Strike*. Was named the Carl Sandburg Home Writer in Residence (2020) in Flat Rock, North Carolina. Is currently an MFA candidate in creative writing at Vermont College of Fine Arts and lives in Hendersonville, North Carolina.

Susan M. Schultz recently retired from the UHM English department. She has 10 books of poetry, including the forthcoming, *Meditations*, from Talisman House. For 24 years, she edited and published Tinfish Press.

Serena Ngaio Simmons (Ngāti Porou) (She/her, he/him) is a queer writer and performer born and raised on the island of Oʻahu. She has a bachelor's degree in English from the University of Hawaiʻi at Mānoa. Digging into such themes as diaspora, identity conflict, queer/takatāpui identity, and home in her writing, her work has been featured in *Tayo Literary Magazine*, *Hawaiʻi Review*, *Flux Magazine*, *Lit Hub*, and *Ora Nui*.

Cory Kamehanaokalā Holt Taum is a Hawaiian artist that lives and works in Hawaiʻi. An active mural artist and cultural practitioner sourcing his inspiration from stories and teachings of the past and their relevance in today's drastically changing Hawaiʻi, his work reflects his fascination with the masterful, bold, and powerful visual forms and patterns developed by the original people here. He is best known for his iconic paintings on a wide range of surfaces, from rusted metal and moss-covered concrete to invasive albizia trees, chosen as his canvases to encourage viewers to question the current state of urbanization and its effect on the health of the land and people of Hawai'i. He has worked on numerous large-scale community murals as well as participated in multiple artist-in-residencies and international mural festivals throughout the Pacific.

Liz Tenrai was born and raised on O'ahu and is a recent Harvard graduate who wrote a poetry thesis supervised by Josh Bell. Her poems are dedicated to her grandmother. Liz currently lives in Cambridge, Massachusetts, where she thinks a lot about cultural survivance, diaspora, and decolonization. She hopes to fight for climate justice in the years ahead.

Delaina Thomas: These two poems have links to Palama Settlement. One is about my Baban, Kame Higa Kaneshiro, who raised her nine children on Auld Lane. She continues to inspire me 38 years after her passing. The poem about George Ka'anana refers to his status as Senior Grandmaster of Kajukenbo, a mixed martial art founded in Palama Settlement in the 1940s. Beloved around the world for his humility and expertise, George passed away in April 2021.

Travis Kaululā'au Thompson (aka TravisT) is an award-winning Kanaka Korean spoken word poet and touring teaching artist from Kalihi, Honolulu, O'ahu, Hawai'i. As the only child of activist educators, he began performing his poetry at protest rallies and political demonstrations in the year 2000. A fixture in the Honolulu spoken word poetry community since 2003, he was a cofounder of the re:VERSES Poetry Collective; cofounder and director for the celebrated local youth literacy non-profit known as Youth Speaks Hawai'i, Pacific Tongues; and is currently a founding member of the Chinatown spoken arts collective known as the HI Poets Society.

"Da Pidgin Guerrilla" **Lee A. Tonouchi**'s most recentest book wuz his children's picture book *Okinawan Princess: Da Legend of Hajichi Tattoos* (Bess Press) with artist Laura Kina, that won one 2020 Skipping Stones Honor Award. His Pidgin poetry collection *Significant Moments in da Life of Oriental Faddah and Son* (Bess) won da 2013 Association for Asian American Studies Book Award. His oddah books include his Pidgin short story collection *Da Word* (Bamboo Ridge Press), his Pidgin essay collection *Living Pidgin* (Tinfish), *Da Kine Dictionary* (Bess), and *Buss Laugh* (Bess). He had a buncha plays produced before by Kumu Kahua Theatre, da Honolulu Theatre for Youth, and East West Players. An' den he's also one food critic for frolichawaii.com.

Maikaʻi Tubbs utilizes found detritus to create sculptures and installations around themes of obsolescence, consumption, and ecology. He regards discarded objects as untapped resources and transforms them to reveal a world of hidden, limitless potential. His process-oriented work reflects honest observations of unnatural familiarity influenced by the blurred boundaries between organic and artificial life. Tubbs is from Honolulu, Hawaiʻi and lives in Brooklyn, New York. He received his BFA in Painting from the UHM and his MFA in Fine Arts from Parsons The New School for Design. When he is not out collecting and hoarding trash, you can find him in or along the nearest body of water. makaitubbs.com or Instagram @maikaitubbs

Briana Koani Uʻu is a graduate of the University of Hawaiʻi at Mānoaʻs English Masterʻs program. No Waikane mai ʻo ia, she is from the ahupuaʻa of Waikane and currently resides in Honolulu. As a kanaka maoli writer, she strives to create stories that represent, validate, and recognize the lives and experiences of her fellow kanaka maoli in all their intricacies, complexities, and multiplicities. She is currently a teacher at Waiʻanae High School.

Doug Upp: This is the second book I'm in, following 2019's "Hustling Verse: An Anthology of Sex Workers' Poetry." Prior to that, there's photocopied fanzines me and my friends made. Maybe a few full-color mags . . . . After decades doing drags in punk bands (Imminent Riot, Patty Judy & The Dirt), on klub dancefloors (House of Chandelier), theatre environments (Taurie Kinoshita's Cruel Theatre), hosting my public access talk show (Shaka Talk), even in a few film fest shorts (HUFF, Unity Crayons, SF Sex Worker Film & Arts Festival), I ain't dressed upp for years now. I'm feeling that freaky fever! Call me whatcha like, and I'll thank you in advance, for lipstick, liner, lashes, a Sharpie & Clearasil! Maybe some Mary Jane, and a mango Monster. Mahalo.

Mahealani Perez Wendt has published in *Bamboo Ridge*; *UCLA Indigenous Peoples' Journal of Law, Culture & Resistance*; *Mānoa*; *Literary Arts Hawaiʻi*; *ʻŌiwi: A Native Hawaiian Journal*; *Kaimana*; *Hawaiʻi Review*; *Oʻahu Review*; *Many Mountains Moving*; *Whetu Moana*; *Effigies: An Anthology of New Indigenous Writing, Pacific Rim*; and *FLUX: The Current of Hawaiʻi magazine*. Her book of poetry, *Uluhaimālama*, was published in 2007. She co-edited *Hoʻolauleʻa: Celebrating 10 Years of Pacific Writing*. Recent work appears in Norton anthologies edited by Poet Laureate Joy Harjo, *When the Light of the World Was Subdued, Our Songs Came Through* (2020) and *Living Nations, Living Words* (2021).

Wooden Wave: See **Matthew Kawika Ortiz**